Once upon a Droshky

Jerome
Charyn

———

Once upon a Droshky

McGraw-Hill Book Company
New York   Toronto   London

The author would like to thank
Norman Podhoretz, Thomas Goethals,
James Shenton, Marie Liburdi,
Candida Donadio, and the late
George Nobbe for their kindness
at a time when it was most needed.

This book is for
Robert Gutwillig
and Andrew Chiappe

Contents

Once upon a Droshky

Finally we lost her. I watched her die. She had lived like a woman of talents and intelligence; she died like a philosopher. I may say that she made the Catholic religion seem beautiful to me, by the serenity of heart with which she fulfilled its instructions, without either carelessness or affectation. She was of a serious nature. Toward the end of her illness she displayed a sort of gaiety too unbroken to be assumed, which was merely a counterpoise to her melancholy condition, the gift of her reason. She only kept her bed for the last two days, and continued to converse quietly with everyone to the last. Finally, when she could no longer talk and was already in her death agony, she broke wind loudly. "Good," she said, turning over, "a woman who can fart is not dead." Those were the last words she spoke.

ROUSSEAU

1.

Second Avenue

You should have a son like I have a son! And
then you would know. "Irving," I say to him, "Irving,
you're a lawyer, a big shot. To you they will listen." But
go talk to a stone. "Pop," he says, "Pop, the building is
being condemned. So what can I do?"

"Do?" And right away I raise one eyebrow. I always
do that when I want attention. That's my trade. I'm an
actor, on the stage and off. "Do? You can do plenty."

And then he begins to moan. All right, they say he's
a genius in court, but let me tell you, I never saw such
a weakling in all my life. After all, I should know. I'm
his father, no?

"Pop, Pop, even a special decree from the President
couldn't save this house. The building is being con-

13

demned, that's final. There's rats on every floor. The toilets never work. Every time it rains there's a flood. Pop? Please."

"No. I'm not moving out. You shouldn't ask me again."

"Pop, how will it look when I run for the Assembly with my father in jail?"

"So save the house! Irving, have a heart. For fifty years already I'm living on Second Avenue. Now I should move out?" I'm ready to put on a performance for Irving, and I start to take out my handkerchief, but I figure to myself that maybe it's better to wait and save the tears for later. "Irving, how will I be able to face anybody? Don't worry, I told them, my Irving will save the house. He's a champion. Let them send a hundred Goliaths after us. Irving will win. So what should I tell them now? You backed off without a fight. Irving, where will Mrs. Moskowitz go? Who will take her in? It's a trick, Irving. Farbstein wants to raise the rent, that's all. Speak to him. He's afraid of you. He knows if you catch him in court it's the end for him. Buy him off, who cares! So the toilets don't work, big deal! Irving, do you remember how many times you and Sonny Shapiro used to look for rats under the stairs, heh? Then you didn't complain."

"Pop, please, who has time? I have to be in court. Are you moving out or not?"

"No!" I can see the situation is getting a little dangerous, and I figure to myself that now is the time to act. So I take out my handkerchief, count to three, and start to cry. "Go raise sons? So they can throw you over in your old age. Only God knows!"

But my little exhibition is interrupted. Farbstein comes

in. You can spot him for a landlord even from a mile away. Here he is with his wrinkled collar and his dirty hands and the little black book that he carries with him wherever he goes.

Me he ignores, but to Irving he walks over and says hello. And I can see right away that something is wrong. When Farbstein doesn't curse or threaten you, then you know you're in trouble. *"Nu?"* he says to Irving. "Any progress?" And I'm waiting for Irving to give it to him, but Irving shrugs his shoulders and doesn't say a word. And now I know the story. Farbstein bought Irving off. A son should sell out his own father, this I never heard!

Farbstein smells victory right away. But I can see, he's still a little worried. Irving maybe he can buy off, but not me! "Yankel," he warns me, "I have two policemen waiting outside." He shows me with his fingers. "Two." And then he motions to Irving. "Tell him, Irving, the law is the law." And Irving is too ashamed even to look me in the face. "Pop," he says, "Pop." What is he now, Farbstein's a stooge?

"Yankel," Farbstein says, "I don't want any trouble, you hear? You're the ringleader. When they see you move out, then they'll all move out. I'm giving you three hours. Irving is my witness. And then I'm sending for the two policemen. Yankel."

"Farbstein," I say, "when did I ever give you permission to call me by my first name, hah?" And then I move a step away from him. "Even the rats and the roaches here hate your guts."

"Irving," he says, "do I have to stand for insults? And in my own house yet. Three hours, Irving, that's all. And then out he goes." Farbstein opens his black book, writes down two or three words with a greasy pencil, and then he walks out. And I'm ready to hiss at him.

"Pop," Irving says, slapping his sides.

I don't answer him even. "Pop," he says three more times. I don't say a word. Then he slaps his sides again. And now I'm ready to give it to him. "Stooge!"

Irving steps back a little. "Stooge." It's worse than a slap in the face. "I said it and I mean it. Stooge. Skunk. *Schlemiel*. There isn't a name you don't deserve."

He takes out his handkerchief and starts wiping his face. It happens every time. Whenever Irving is in trouble, right away he reaches for his handkerchief. "Pop."

One word he knows. *Pop!*

"Walk away from me, Irving. From this moment on I'm disowning you." Sure, it's easy to say. I haven't got a dime to my name. And without Irving I wouldn't be able to stay alive for a week. But I say it again. "You hear me, Irving, you're no more my son."

His whole face begins to crumple up like a prune. I feel sorry for him myself.

"Pop, please. I'm running for the Assembly. Who can afford to make enemies? Farbstein knows all the District Leaders. What can I do? The building is being condemned. Pop, you want me to lose the election? Pop?"

"Irving, don't beg. Elections, elections. Irving, you used to be a Samson. Look at you now, you're a regular shrimp! Farbstein you picked out for a partner yet. You used to spit on people like that. All right, win your election. Yankel's moving out!"

"Pop," he says, "you won't be sorry. And the place I picked out for you, Pop, you'll kiss me for it."

"I said I'm moving out, but from me, Irving, don't expect any kisses."

"You'll see, Pop, you'll see. I'll be back before five." And then he straightens out his tie, picks up his brief case, and now he's ready to go to court. If those other lawyers only knew Irving the way I know Irving, they wouldn't be afraid of him for a minute. "Pop, you'll see."

"Irving, so get off the stage already, go!"

And after Irving leaves I go right down to Mrs. Moskowitz. I hear somebody shouting. Farbstein's inside, I know it right away. I'm ready for some action. All right, so I've lost the war already, but at least let me win one little battle. The door is open and I walk in without announcing myself. What, I have to be formal? I know Tillie Moskowitz for almost fifty years. Tillie is sitting in the kitchen and she's crying. Farbstein is shaking his fist at her. "Remember," he says, "nobody can help you now. I'll tell them to throw all your furniture out in the street." And he puts down a piece of paper on the kitchen table and tells her to sign.

"Sign?" she says. "What should I sign?" And Tillie picks up the paper, puts on her glasses and starts to read. "What is this? LET IT BE KNOWN THAT THE UNDERSIGNED HEREBY TERMINATES—— What kind of talk is this? I never heard from such words."

"Sign it," Farbstein says, "or I'm sending for the police."

And when Tillie hears the word *police*, right away she begins to shake and she's ready to sign. And that's when I make my entrance. If only somebody had written a part for me like this, I would have been the biggest star on Second Avenue!

"Tillie," I say, "don't sign!"

And now it's Farbstein who starts shaking, and then he grabs up the paper and puts it inside his pocket.

"Tillie," I say, "look, I trapped a rat." And I walk over to Farbstein. "So show me, Farbstein, show me what's written on the paper. And then I'll tell Tillie if she should sign." And now I know how Irving feels when he's winning a case in court. "Well, Farbstein, I'm waiting."

"Yankel," he says, and by now his eyes are narrowed down to two slits and it looks like some poison is ready to shoot right out of them. "I'll fix you for good. Irving or no Irving." This time he writes a whole sentence down in his black book, and while he's writing he looks back and forth at Tillie and me. And for a second the two slits spread apart and his eyes glow and dance and roll around like two balls of fire. Honest to God, I'm afraid of him myself. But I should show a snake and a snotnose like Farbstein that I'm afraid, never in my life! "Out, Farbstein," I say, "or you will remember this day for the rest of your life." And Farbstein, without having time even to put his black book away, retreats.

"Yankel," Tillie says, "you told him off. You should be the lawyer, not Irving!" And I take one look at her and tears come to my eyes. The left side of her face is pushed in, the skin hangs down from her neck like a rooster or a goat, both of her legs are swollen, and everywhere you look there's a blister or a bump showing out. Tillie, Tillie, only forty years ago she was the beauty of East Broadway. And believe me, I had my sessions with her before she married Moskowitz the furrier, and after too! I'm telling you, there will never be another Tillie!

But look at her now! What can I do, memories are memories. For me she'll always be Tillie of East Broadway even with her pushed-in face. Sure, laugh, you see the blisters and the veins, but I remember the breasts that used to stand out like plump potato blintzes. 'Tillie,' I want to say, 'do you remember the time when the cat crawled through the window and started to howl and you thought it was Moskowitz who sent the cat to spy on us and you wouldn't get undressed until I made a Frankenstein face and chased it out?' What's the use? Where, she would say, when? Me, I remember everything. With me nothing dies. A slap on the face from my father fifty years ago and I can still feel the sting today. So, whoever you are, if you threw a cup of coffee in my face in Schimmel's Cafeteria in 1923 don't expect me to shake hands now and forgive. Do something to me, that's the way I am. And can you blame me if I try to look out for Tillie? Say I'm sentimental, call me a *schlemiel,* kill me if you want, but don't expect me to change.

"Yankel," Tillie says, "you saved the house for us."

Should I lie to her? No! "Tillie, the house is lost. I'm moving out myself."

"Yankel," she says, "you mean it? And what about Irving?"

Should I tell her that Irving sold us out? No! After all, a son is still a son. But that's not the reason why I don't tell her. I'm not trying to protect Irving. Why should I become a hypocrite in my old age? You want to hear the truth, I'm too ashamed to tell her.

"Irving?" I say. "So what can Irving do? The law is the law. Ask Farbstein, he'll tell you. Even Irving can't win against the law."

"So where should I go, Yankel? An *alte* like me?"

"Don't worry, Tillie, Irving will find a place for all of us. What, you think otherwise I would agree to move out?"

"Yankel." And I know already what she's going to say. "Yankel, everything comes out in the end. God is punishing me now for being a *bumekah*."

"Bumekah?" I say. "Who, who was a bumekah? Tillie, Tillie. Shaindele Goldstein, *she* was a bumekah. Faigele, the grocer's wife, another bumekah. But Tillie, believe me, *you* were not a bumekah. Tillie, after all, I didn't meet you in the street. I knew you long before you were married to Moskowitz. Am I right or am I wrong?"

And then she looks at me, and I swear to God, underneath the wrinkles and the bumps, she's blushing. "Yankel," she says, "not only you. I didn't go away to the mountains for week ends with Hymie the painter when Moskowitz—let him rest in peace—went to visit his sister in New Jersey? Maybe three times."

"Tillie," I say, and I try to look surprised. "Hymie the painter? This I never new." Sure I knew, but I didn't want to spoil her little secret. Hymie used to sit in Schimmel's Cafeteria all day and talk about his romance with Tillie.

But wait, she's not finished yet. "And Max," she says, "the manager from the Art Theatre—he should also rest in peace—another boy friend. I could tell you plenty."

"Max the manager?" This I never knew! That monkey, it's a lucky thing for him he's no longer alive, or I would make it so hot for him he would have to lay low for a month. For twenty years he sat in the same seat at

Schimmel's and about Tillie he never mentioned a word. No wonder he would forget to show up at the theatre three or four times every month. Where's Max, everybody would ask, and nobody could say! Now it's no longer a mystery.

"Yankel," she says, "now you believe me? I'm a bumekah."

So why should I make her feel bad? "Tillie, *shah!* Hymie the painter, he was handsome like a prince. Half the women on Second Avenue would have given up their lives for a chance to go away with him for a week end." Was that man ugly! He had a nose like a trumpet and a chin like a spike. Children would run from him when they saw him in the street. "And Max. Tillie, all the manufacturers' wives used to run after him." Sure, the only things that would ever run after Max the manager were bedbugs, beetles, and lice. The man never took a bath in his life! "Tillie a bumekah, no! This I can guarantee. God should strike me down, Tillie, if I'm telling you a lie. Never once in fifty years did I ever hear anyone call Tillie Moskowitz a bumekah." And for once I'm not telling a lie. All right, other names they called her, but never bumekah.

"Tillie, you shouldn't worry. What, you think I'm going to let a snotnose like Farbstein rule over me? Stay here. If Farbstein comes around again, don't let him in. And Tillie, if he should catch you out in the hall, remember, don't sign anything."

"Yankel," she says, "I knew I wouldn't have to worry with you around," and she closes one eye and makes herself ready for a kiss. What, I should refuse my Tillie a kiss? Never! So I look all over her face for a place to kiss, and everywhere I see either a blister or a bump. "Tillie, who has time for kisses? I have to save the house!"

And now I go and make the rounds. I knock on Mendel the merchant's door. "Mendel," I say, but *Mendel* is not enough. You could knock on his door for a lifetime and he wouldn't answer you until you say, *Mendel, Mendel the merchant*. Some merchant! He used to drag a pushcart up and down Orchard Street. And what did he have to sell? A rotten tomato, a broken bracelet, or a deck of pinochle cards with half the aces missing. Even when he was working he was always on relief. But who wants to stand forever outside his door? So let him be Mendel the merchant. I should worry. I knock again. "Mendele. Mendel the merchant." And right away he opens up the door.

"Yankel," he says. "Oy, I thought it was the police. Come in, come in." And you should see his place. It's worse than a junkyard. Everywhere is piled old tire tubes, dented pots, blankets with holes in them bigger than your fists, coats and hats from before the Russian Revolution. Just ask and Mendel has it! And his pushcart, it sits in the middle of the room with a missing wheel and a broken handle, like a monument or a trophy. The wood is beginning to rot through and through and any day an army of termites will show up and eat it up alive. But go tell it to Mendel. I think he would die on the spot if somebody took away his pushcart. Tillie tells me that Mendel sleeps in it all the time, but this I don't believe. After all, there's a limit to everything. I turn around and look at Mendel. His whole face starts to glow, and right away I know he wants to sell me something.

"Yankel," he says, "maybe you need a blanket?" He knows what I'm going to tell him, so he doesn't even wait for an answer. "Yankel, what about a coffee pot, first class! I mean it, without a scratch or a dent. I polish it every day myself with a piece of steel wool." And now he starts arguing with himself, and then he says to me, "No, why should I lie? The coffee pot is not for you. The nozzle is a little bent. It drips, the coffee pot. To Fishbein, that low-life, I would sell it. But not to you. Wait, Yankel, wait. For you I have something special. Wait." And then he disappears for a minute, and he comes back holding an ugly copper pot with a rusty faucet. He rubs the pot with both hands and his eyes start to twinkle, and I think to myself, who knows, maybe there's a genie inside? With Mendel's merchandise everything is possible. "Yankel," he says, "a beauty, no?"

"So tell me, what is it?"

And right away his eyes stop twinkling and his face turns a little gray. He starts scolding himself. "Mendel, Mendel, go and do business with a fool. . . . Yankel, tell me, you never saw a samovar in your life?"

"This, this is a *samovar?*" Honest to God, it looks more like an old-time chamber pot!

"Yankel, believe me, it's a treasure. With this samovar you will brew a glass tea like you never tasted in your life."

"Mendel, please, put it away."

"Yankel, listen. This samovar that I am holding in my hands now once belonged to Rasputin himself. With the help of the samovar he poisoned three ministers, two monks, and a king. Yankel, don't be a *schlimazel*. Such a samovar, how can you refuse? Take it. Yankel, yes?"

"No."

He takes the samovar and puts it on top of a pile of tire tubes. And now the samovar sits with the rusty lip of the faucet pointing crookedly in Mendel's direction. Mendel puts his hands in his lumpy pockets and talks to himself. I know, I spoiled the day for him. But what can I do? Who would drink tea from such a rusty pot. Only Rasputin! "Mendel," I say, "did you find a place yet?"

"Place? What for should I find a place?"

"Mendel, the house is coming down. We all have to move out."

His lips begin to twitch. "Yankel, you told me yourself maybe a million times that Irving would save for us the house." He leans against the pile of tire tubes for a minute and the samovar begins to shake. "Yankel."

So what can I tell him? Should I say, Mendel, my Irving is worse than Farbstein yet! And the way he looks at me, like I'm the last hope he has left in the world. "Mendele, everything will be all right, you'll see."

"Yankel," he says, "do something for me, please." And now he stands near the pushcart and holds on to the broken handle for support. Poor Mendel, I saw him many times when the police chased after him with summonses, or when one or two of Fishbein's goons turned over his pushcart, but I never saw him so frightened like this.

"Mendel, you know I'll try for you. But Mendel, if worse comes to worse, the City will find another apartment for —."

"No," he says, "no. Who'll help me move out my merchandise, *heh?* And without my merchandise I don't take a step. Yankel, everything I have is here. Who could get used to another place? When I pull the chain on top of the toilet and I hear the water fill up, this to me is music. And when I talk to the wall, it talks back. I should *plotz* if I'm telling you a lie. So how can I move out? Put me in a palace even and I could never call it my home."

"Mendel, I know. But Farbstein has all the big shots on his side. Who knows, maybe even the Mayor is working for him? But Mendel, I'll try. Meanwhile, if Farbstein comes around again, don't make trouble. Mendel, you hear?"

"Yankel, when did Mendel the merchant ever make trouble for anybody?"

"What, you didn't throw a shoe at Farbstein's head when he came around last month for the rent?"

"One shoe, I threw ten shoes! And if I had another ten, I would have thrown them too. But *he* made the trouble, not Mendel. 'Move, Mendel, move,' he tells me, 'before I throw you out.' Yankel, this is the way to talk to a tenant? All right, the City pays for me the rent, but he still gets every penny just the same. So tell me, Yankel, I was wrong to throw the shoes at him?"

"Who says you were wrong? But this is not the question. Mendel, lay low. He could have you locked up. Make me a promise. No more shoes."

He looks up at the ceiling, slaps himself over the head, then he talks to the pushcart for a minute, and finally he says, "All right, Yankel, no more shoes!"

And now I go across the hall to see Morris the musician. They both live on the same floor, but when you go from Mendel to Morris it's like changing off from night to day. They have only one thing in common: they're both on relief. But what can you expect from Morris, he's a music teacher. And when did you ever hear of a music teacher who wasn't on relief? But it's a pleasure to talk to Morris, I mean it. Morris is a gentleman. Not like Mendel! Morris doesn't curse or shout or throw shoes. And can that man play the fiddle! Regular concerts he used to give in Schimmel's Cafeteria, and for free! So let Yascha Heifetz or Yehudi Menuhin play in Carnegie Hall, I'll sit better in Schimmel's and listen to Morris.

"Morris," I say, and I don't even knock on the door. Who wants to disturb him? Maybe he doesn't hear me? "Morris," I say, a little louder. And then I knock two, three times on the door. And now I hear him coming. He opens the door and looks outside.

"Morris," I say, "you're busy with the fiddle? I'll come back later."

"Yankel?" he says. "I thought maybe it was Mendel. The man never leaves me alone. Just like a leech. He knocks on my door every five minutes with something new to sell. Yankel, so why are you standing out in the hall? Come inside, please. I'll make you a glass of tea." See, I told you, a regular gentleman. Mendel wouldn't offer you a glass of tea even if your tongue was hanging out. And maybe Morris is on relief, but at least he has a table and a few chairs. In Mendel's apartment you can't even find a place to sit down.

"Yankel, a slice of lemon with your tea?"

What a question! Who could drink tea without lemon, only a *goy* or a barbarian like Mendel!

So we sit and drink tea.

"Morris," I say, "you heard the bad news?"

"Bad news?" Morris says, and with his fingers he starts sweeping the rinds from the lemon towards the edge of the table.

"About the house. Irving can't do a thing. We all have to move out."

"Yankel, for me it's not a tragedy. I'll find another place. And wherever I go I'll take with me my teapot and my fiddle and I'm a happy man. No, Yankel?"

"You're absolutely right. About you or me I'm not worried, but with Tillie and Mendel it's a different story. Morris, you were by Schimmel's this morning?"

"Yankel, today's a special day? You know every morning I'm in Schimmel's rain or shine, so why do you ask?"

"Fishbein was there?"

"Yankel, please, don't look for trouble. If Irving can't help, what can Fishbein do?"

And now I stand up. "Morris, I asked you a question, so give me the answer. He was there?"

"Sure he was there. Two tables he took over for himself. He should only *plotz!*"

This is the first time in my life that I ever heard Morris curse.

"Morris," I say, "tell me, Fishbein ever did something to you?"

He doesn't answer. He takes the lemon rinds from the table and drops them inside a paper bag. Morris must be a little annoyed. He doesn't even offer me another glass of tea. "Yankel," he says, "how can you like such a gangster!"

"Morris, when you want a favor, you go to Fishbein. Fishbein never refuses."

"Yankel, please, don't even mention his name." He takes the teapot off the stove. I can see already, he wants me to go. I hear a knock on the door.

"Hide," Morris says. "Yankel, if it's Farbstein, I don't want him to know that you're here."

"Morris, since when are you so afraid for Farbstein? Why should I hide?"

"There always has to be a reason? Just because!"

"Because," I say, "for me *because* is not enough," and I open up the door. It's not Farbstein, it's Mendel. It's dark in the hall, and for a minute he thinks he's talking to Morris.

"Morris," he says, "I have for you something special. A samovar that belonged to Czar Nicholas himself. You believe me? I can show you proof even. Where could you get such a bargain? Morris, let me in, please. Imagine, boiling tea from the same samovar with the czars!" And now he recognizes me, and he puts the samovar behind his back. "Yankel, I thought it was Morris. Goodbye." And his face looks so gray, that I'm ready to take out a dollar and buy his samovar on the spot. "Wait, Mendele, wait." But he disappears.

And now Morris walks over to the door. "See," he says, "a regular *nudnik*. It's lucky for me you were here. Otherwise he would have chased me all over the house. So tell me, Yankel, what did he want to sell me now?"

"Nothing special. A rusty pot."

"A pot? Is this a Mendel! Nobody knows how much I stand from him. A pot yet!"

Morris keeps talking, but I walk outside. He's so busy with himself, it takes him two minutes before he notices that I'm no longer there. "Yankel," he calls down from the second floor, "where are you going?"

"Where else? To Schimmel's!"

A cop is standing outside the house, so I stay in the hall

for a minute. Who is Farbstein after now? Tillie, Mendel, Morris, or me? The cop walks across the street, so I figure to myself that it's safe, and I go outside. I see Mendel standing near the window. His back is stooped over and one of his ears stick out and he looks just like a spook. I want to call up to him, 'Mendel, Mendel,' but who can wait around with a cop across the street? So I run over to Schimmel's.

Schimmel is dead now twenty years but his son is Schimmel number two! He looks like Schimmel, he talks like Schimmel, he *is* Schimmel! After Schimmel died, everyone went around with a funeral face. You think we were mourning for Schimmel? No! We were mourning for the Cafeteria! "It's a catastrophe," Morris said, "what will we do without the Cafeteria?" Who could answer such a question? So we waited for Schimmel's to close down. "Yankel," Morris asked me, "did they take out the fixtures yet?" No. "Did Farbstein buy off the mortgage? Schmulka tells me he wants to tear down the walls and build there a market." But nobody came to tear down the walls. There was a lock on the door but inside everything was the same. And then, a week after the funeral, Tillie came over to me and her whole body was shaking. "Yankel," she said, "did you see him?" Who? What? "Go," and she dragged me over to Schimmel's. The lock was off the door, but everybody was waiting outside. "Yankel," Morris said, "he came back from the grave." Even Fishbein was afraid. "What's the commotion?" I said, and then I went inside. Schmulka, Schimmel's cashier, was standing behind the counter.

"Schmulka," I said, "who are you working for now?"

"Schimmel," he said.

"Schmulka, you want a shoe in the head?" And he knew I meant business.

"Yankel, wait . . . if Schimmel has a son, then the son is also a *Schimmel,* no?"

"Don't talk riddles, Schmulka."

"Honest to God, Yankel, I'm working now for Schimmel's son."

"Schimmel had a son?"

"I know, Yankel, it's a mystery. But here he is," and he pointed to the room behind the counter. "And Yankel, he looks more like Schimmel than Schimmel himself." He saw me start to walk behind the counter, and he called me over and whispered in my ear. "Be careful. Every time I see him my stomach starts to jump."

So I walked into the room behind the counter, and there he was, another Schimmel. "My friend," I said to myself, "if you think you're going to frighten me, you're mistaken." I shook his hand and said hello, and then I walked out of the room.

"Yankel," Schmulka said, "you saw him?"

"I saw him."

And then I stood near the door and started to motion with my hands. "Max, Morris, everybody! Come inside. Schimmel's is open again!"

And for weeks after everybody talked only about one thing: Schimmel's son.

"So how could Schimmel have a son? The man wasn't even married!"

"And how do you know he wasn't married?"

"How do I know? I know, that's all! And if this is Schimmel's a son, how come he wasn't at his father's funeral?"

"How come? Could be a hundred reasons. Maybe he was in jail!"

So we talked and shouted and argued back and forth, and we came to only one conclusion: we didn't know the first thing about Schimmel or his son. And this was a little hard for us to accept. When he was alive, Schimmel never took a step outside the Cafeteria. If you wanted him in the morning, or in the afternoon, or even in the middle of the night, you always knew where to find him. If he wasn't sleeping on Schmulka's bench, then he was chewing on a stale roll, or playing solitaire in the little room behind the counter. We had Schimmel all mapped out. We knew every one of his moves. If Schimmel touched the wart on his nose or sat in his room and played solitaire, then we knew business was bad. If Schimmel slapped his head and started complaining, then we knew business was good. And if he went around saying, "Oy, I'm going to have to close down the Cafeteria," then we all knew that he was thinking of adding an extra counter or hiring three more helpers. "You can't trust anybody," Schmulka would say, "not Fishbein, not Max, not Yankel, not Morris, but you can always be sure of Schimmel!" And how did it turn out? Schimmel was the biggest mystery on Second Avenue. Who knows how many sons he had!

But for me one son is enough. I walk into Schimmel's and there he is. He's sitting on Schmulka's broken-down bench and he's picking little pieces off the crust of a three-day-old onion roll with his black fingers until the onion roll is almost bald already. Sometimes I forget that Schimmel the second is not Schimmel the first, and I ask him questions that only his father could have answered.

For example. "Schimmel," I'll say, "you know who I saw yesterday coming out of Gluckstern's? Finkelstein's wife. Kill me, I can't remember her name! Was it Esther or Eda?" And whenever I think about Finkelstein right away I remember the tweed suit that still sits in my closet. You should see a suit! For forty years I've had it, and it fits on me like it was made special for a prince. Where can you find a tailor like Finkelstein today? Itzie Hollander, Jacob Ben-Ami, Yudel Dubinsky, everybody who was *anybody* on Second Avenue ran to Finkelstein to be fitted for a suit. I know it for a fact that Yudel Dubinsky never went on stage unless he was wearing a suit made by Finkelstein himself. And what happened? Maybe thirty years ago Finkelstein's wife went off to Montreal with a carpenter or a salesman—who remembers?—and the tailor hanged himself in his own shop. "So Schimmel," I'll say again, "was it Esther or Eda?" And he'll look at me for a minute and maybe shrug his left shoulder or puff out one of his cheeks and then he'll go back to whatever he was doing. The trouble is that nobody bothers to make a distinction any more between Schimmel the father and Schimmel the son. Half of my friends have already forgotten that Schimmel the first ever died. People are beginning to take Schimmel for granted. Everybody is sure that when *this* Schimmel goes, another Schimmel will show up. I'm not so sure. With Schimmel around, anything can happen.

"Schimmel," I say, "Fishbein's still here?"

He keeps on picking away at the bald onion roll, and without looking up once, he points to the back of the Cafeteria. Meanwhile Schmulka walks over. He winks

to me and starts mimicking Schimmel. "Yankel," he says,
"I hear Farbstein is on the warpath again. Can Irving
do something or not?" I walk with Schmulka to the
back of the Cafeteria. Fishbein is sitting by himself.
"Schmulka," I say, "excuse me for a minute. I have to
talk to Fishbein."

He winks to me again. "I know, I know. If Irving
can't shut up Farbstein, then Fishbein will." And then
he walks over to the counter.

I sit down next to Fishbein. He's drinking tea.

"Fishie," I say, "so how's the leg?"

He dangles his tea bag over the glass.

"The same," he says. Fishbein had a blood clot in his
leg the year before last and now he's practically a cripple.

Morris comes into the Cafeteria. He sees me sitting
with Fishbein and he doesn't even come over to say hello.
All the tables next to us are empty. That's the way it always is when Fishbein is around. People are still afraid
of him. And who can blame them? Thirty years ago Fishbein was the biggest gangster on the whole East Side. He
used to terrorize all the local businessmen. If you didn't
pay him protection, you could forget about your market,
or your store, or your stand. Even Schimmel had to pay
up. Once I saw Fishbein's goons go to work on Bernstein's delicatessen and they threw everything out in the
street, even the salamis. On Second Avenue the name
Fishbein was like a curse. His own mother said the Kaddish for him, and considered him as dead. But there were
still bigger gangsters than Fishbein. And one day—was
it in 1933 or 1934—the word went around that Lepke or
somebody else was out to kill Fishbein. "Good," every-

body said, "now the lion himself will know what it means to be eaten alive." But then we began to reconsider. Good or bad, a Jew is still a Jew, no? So we hid Fishbein for three weeks behind the counter in Schimmel's and we kept him alive on bagels and lox. And then like a miracle Lepke himself was killed and Fishbein came out from behind the counter. And from that day on Fishbein never bothered a soul on Second Avenue. And if some goon from uptown tried to push around one of the merchants or the tailors, right away Fishbein was called in. "Fishie, they want Boris should pay five dollars a week for protection." And Fishbein would say, "Boys, leave it to me." And the goon would never come around again. Then after a few years Fishbein himself went into retirement. Sure, even a gangster can retire! And now he sits in Schimmel's and collects Social Security!

"Fishie," I say, "the situation with Farbstein is not so good. He's getting ready to dispossess the whole house."

Fishbein dangles the tea bag inside the glass. But I know he's listening.

"Fishie, I thought maybe Irving could do something, but it's no use."

I'm waiting for Fishbein to say, "Yankel, you can count on me," but he doesn't say a word. When did you ever hear of Fishbein refusing a favor? But who can blame him? He has problems of his own. It's no joke after having a blood clot in your leg. But I decide to ask him, anyway. "Fishie, maybe you can do something? You know how Farbstein is afraid of you. I don't say you should threaten him or push him around. Who wants violence? Talk to him. That will be enough."

And now he puts down the tea bag. "Yankel, you know

yourself that Irving is working for Farbstein, so how can you ask?"

Should I look angry and deny it? No, not to a friend! "Fishie, I first found out today. That's why I came to you. I thought maybe . . ."

"Yankel, you know if I lean on Farbstein, he'll call for Irving. And who wants to start up with Irving? That's all I need! Irving wants to be Governor. And if he ever catches me in court, he'll crucify me! Yankel, I have to tell you? He's your son!"

"Fishie, who wants to throw you in trouble? I'll find a way to settle with Farbstein myself. One thing, Fishie. Irving has ambitions, I know, but he's not a snake. This I can guarantee. Sure, Irving wants to be the Governor, who says no, but not like that! Fishie, believe me, from my Irving you have nothing to worry." This is what I would like to believe, but who knows if it's true?

And now Fishbein picks up the tea bag again, dangles it nervously for a minute, and then drops it inside the glass. "Yankel, I'm sorry, I can't help you . . . but I know somebody who can."

"So I'm waiting. Who?"

He hesitates for a minute and like a fortune-teller he sticks his nose inside the glass. "Pincus."

I stand up and start to walk away from the table. "Fishie, you know already that when people are around me there is one name that is never mentioned. So why are you starting up?"

"Yankel, he's the only one. Nobody else can help you. Not even Irving can put Pincus down. Yankel, he'll be here soon. Should I talk to him?"

And then like magic in comes Pincus through the door.

Today is Tuesday, so he's wearing his Tuesday suit. Sure, Pincus has seven suits, one for every day of the week. And God forbid, if he should ever wear his Tuesday suit on a Wednesday, or his Wednesday suit on a Friday, I think the world would come to an end. All seven suits were sewn by Finkelstein himself, but even a suit by Finkelstein can't work miracles. Pincus is not even five feet tall, and he has a hump on his back, and a boil on his nose that's almost as big as a grape. But ugly as he is, people can't stay away from him. He's the main attraction at Schimmel's. As soon as he comes in, everybody congregates around him. Why do you think Morris shows up at Schimmel's every afternoon? Because of Pincus!

"Yankel," Fishbein says, "should I ask him?"

"Fishie," I say, "you want to stay my friend?"

Pincus walks over to his table. Right away Schimmel brings over a plate of boiled potatoes and a large bowl of borscht. Schimmel reserves a table all day for Pincus. And even if the Cafeteria is packed, no one is allowed to sit down at the table. Once I saw a man try to remove a salt shaker from Pincus' table, and Schimmel almost had a fit. And Schimmel the first was even worse than Schimmel the second. He worshiped Pincus. He wanted to keep the Cafeteria closed every morning, because Pincus showed up only in the afternoons. "Schimmel," everybody told him, "don't be a dope. Did you ever hear of a cafeteria that was closed in the morning? People will laugh at you. You'll have to close up altogether." But Schimmel wouldn't listen. So me and Morris and Tillie and Itzie the shoemaker formed a special committee to keep Schimmel's open in the morning, and we all agreed that I should be the spokesman. "After all," Morris said, "the only way to get to Schimmel is through Pincus, and the only way to get to Pincus is through Yankel!" Sure, at that time me and Pincus were just like Mutt and Jeff. What, when Pincus dedicated his first book of poems to "*Y R*," you think the *Y R* was for Yetta Rosenberg, the Roumanian actress? That's what Pincus says now, but don't believe it! The *Y R* was for me, *Yankel Rabinowitz*. And if anybody wanted a favor from Pincus, first they came to me. I never liked to bother Pincus about unimportant things, but the situation with Schimmel and the Cafeteria was becoming a little dangerous, so I said, "Pincus, have a heart. For you it's no problem. You're a regular gypsy! You stay up all night and sleep in the morning. But how will the rest of us be able to get through the day without a cup of Schimmel's coffee in the morning. Pincus, we'll never survive!" So Pincus agreed to show up one or two mornings every other week, and now Schimmel was satisfied.

Pincus sits and eats his potatoes and borscht, and everybody brings over their chair. Soon Pincus will finish eating and then Schimmel will close up the counter for half an hour. And when Schmulka leans over to light up Pincus' cigar, the whole Cafeteria knows it's time to keep quiet. And God forbid, if now Wolf the wholesaler should try to tune up his balalaika or maybe whisper to Morris, Schmulka will throw him out by his ear, and poor Wolf will be banished from Schimmel's for at least a week. When Pincus speaks, no one is allowed to make a sound.

And now Schimmel is getting ready to close up the

counter, and I can see that Fishbein wants to go over to Pincus' table. He keeps playing with the tea bag, but he looks at Pincus all the time.

"Fishie," I say, "you're making me nervous. Go over already!"

But Fishbein doesn't want to leave me by myself, so he says, "Yankel, I'll listen from here."

"Am I a baby that you have to sit with me? Go!"

"Yankel," he says, "we'll talk later." Fishbein's left leg is still a little swollen from the blood clot, and he walks with a limp. He takes three steps, then he turns around and says, "Yankel, don't worry. I'll find a way to fix Farbstein." Schmulka is getting ready to light up the cigar, and now Fishbein drags his left leg and hurries over to Pincus' table. Fishbein knows that Schimmel would never dare to throw him out of the Cafeteria, but he still wants to get over to the table on time. Schmulka makes a place for him, and Fishbein sits down. And now I'm the only outcast in the whole Cafeteria. But no one is forcing me to sit in the corner. If I wanted I could go over and sit next to Fishbein, but why should I? Pincus is the man who ruined my career! And for what? Everybody on Second Avenue knows the story. That midget over there fell in love with Shaindele Goldstein, so it's my fault? And who was Shaindele? A chorus girl in one of Molly Picon's shows! He used to send her flowers, write poems to her, and chase after her like a dog, but what did she want with a midget like that! I don't want to be a show-off, but why shouldn't I tell the truth? Pincus ran after Shaindele, and Shaindele, she ran after me! But Pincus was my friend, so I tried to avoid her. And every time I had a chance, I would talk to him. "Pincus, a chorus girl? Everybody is

laughing at you!" But the minute I said a bad word about
her, he would throw me out of his room. And Shaindele,
she wouldn't leave me alone! She said she would kill herself unless I went with her to the Catskills for a week. So
what could I do? I had to agree! And what was my reward? Pincus found out, and the same day Shaindele and
me came back from the Catskills, he caught me in Schimmel's and spit right in my face. And in front of everybody yet! And this was only the beginning. At that time
Pincus used to write reviews for the Yiddish newspapers
and magazines, and all the actors and the producers were
afraid of him. Sure, a show could never be a success on
Second Avenue unless Pincus gave his approval. And
now every time I read the *Forward* or the *Day,* I would
see my name mentioned in one of Pincus' articles or reviews. He called me a fake, a fish-seller, a toad without
talent. What, what didn't he call me! The producers didn't
dare to put me in a show. They knew that if I were in
a show, Pincus would automatically call it a bomb. Nobody, not even the Hebrew Actors' Union, could do
something for me. And when Maurice Schwartz told me
himself that he couldn't take me to California with the
Yiddish Art Theatre to do *Yashe Kalb,* I knew for me it
was the end. So you expect me to come out from my corner, heh? Better I'll sit here forever than go over and listen to one of Pincus' stories!

And now everybody is waiting. Will Pincus talk about
the Yiddish Art Theatre, or about the life of Sholem
Aleichem, or will he talk about Lermontov's duel, or
Gogol's trip to Palestine? Only Pincus himself knows!
But whatever story he decides to tell—let it be about a
peddler in the street—one thing is sure: Pincus will be-

witch the whole Cafeteria. And everybody will sit around him like little children at a puppet show. But how can you compare a puppet to Pincus? Sure, a puppet can dance and sing and work all kinds of wonders with its wooden legs, but even if the greatest genius in the world were pulling its strings and faking its voice, it could never in its life tell a story like Pincus. This I can guarantee!

I can hear Pincus from my table. He mentions the name Turgenev. So I know today he will tell the story of Turgenev and the prima donna—who can remember her name? Pincus has told this story maybe a hundred times, but Morris, and Schimmel, and Schmulka, and everybody else in the Cafeteria will tuck in their behinds and wait for Pincus to tell the same story again. If Pincus were a professional story-teller, half the Cafeteria would fall asleep on him and the other half would look at him with empty faces. Sure, Pincus would have a special routine, and pretty soon Morris and everybody else would get to know all of his little tricks, and in time Pincus himself would become bored by his own stories. And then, God forbid, if Pincus wanted to talk about Turgenev, the whole Cafeteria would rebel. "Oh, no," Morris would say, "not Turgenev again!" And maybe Schimmel would stamp his foot, and Schmulka would chase Pincus out of the Cafeteria. But this is not the case. Pincus is not a professional, he's not a showman, he's a genuine one-hundred-dred-per-cent story-teller. If Schimmel sits with his eyes ready to pop out, it's not because Pincus moved his fingers and mumbled some fancy mumbo jumbo. Pincus doesn't practice voodoo. And it's not because he has learned the art of telling a story. If that's all it was, believe me, Schimmel would be snoring by now. It's because

Pincus himself is always moved by his own stories. If Pincus cries when he tells the story of how Pushkin died, it's not because he is trying to impress the Cafeteria. Schmulka and Morris would never stand for crocodile tears. Other story-tellers have tried it, and they've been banned from Schimmel's for life. Pincus cries because he loves Pushkin. And he mourns for all the wonderful poems and stories that Pushkin would have written if he had lived at least for another five years. And it's like a disease. Soon the whole Cafeteria will be crying too. "Pushkin is my brother," Schimmel will say, after he dries his face and puts away his handkerchief. "From now on we will leave an empty chair for him in the Cafeteria." Now you know why there are always seven empty chairs in the Cafeteria. The whole world burns candles, but Schimmel leaves empty chairs. One for Pushkin, one for Lermontov, one for Turgenev, one for Lev Tolstoy, one for Gorky, one for Peretz, and one for Jacob Gordin, the Jewish playwright. Pincus' seven favorites.

So you should know, if Pincus is going to talk about Turgenev and the opera singer, he has a good reason for it. Who knows? Maybe he was reading a book by Turgenev last night? Or maybe on the way to the Cafeteria he was thinking about something in his own life, and it reminded him of Turgenev? But whatever the reason, when Pincus tells the story now, you will know more about Turgenev than you could learn from reading a hundred books. Not because Pincus is an encyclopedia. Sure, he makes plenty of mistakes. He forgets names and dates, and sometimes from the way he tells the story you will think that Turgenev lived to be two hundred years old. But is that such a terrible crime? The important thing is that Pincus will make Turgenev come alive for you, and while Pincus is talking you will think that Turgenev himself is sitting next to you in Schimmel's. Maybe Pincus *is* a sorcerer. Sit in Schimmel's and he will conjure up for you Pushkin, Gogol, Hymie the fish peddler, anybody!

I can see, Schimmel is laughing already under his breath. He would never dare to make a sound. The whole Cafeteria would censor him. Even Fishbein, who never smiles, is smiling. That's the power that Pincus has! And now Pincus talks a little louder. Is he trying to make sure that I can hear him? Pincus never looks at me once, but the whole time I feel that he is talking only to me. Sitting by myself in the corner *I* am his audience, and not the *nudniks* who are bunched around him. Could be I'm an idiot, but that's the way I feel. Pincus is trying to woo me with his voice. And I stay in my corner and pretend that I'm unimpressed. Not a muscle in my face moves. And meanwhile Pincus' face is beginning to light up like a jack-o'-lantern. Last year I caught the flu and I had to stay in bed for a week. And when Morris came around to give me the news he told me that for the whole week Pincus wasn't Pincus. He faltered when he spoke, and his stories were terrible. And he didn't even show up at Schimmel's for the last three days. The whole Cafeteria was worried. Schimmel was getting diarrhea already. And the same day I came back to the Cafeteria, Pincus came back too. Could be it's a coincidence, who knows? Pincus told everybody that his favorite aunt had died. But I know for a fact that he never had a "favorite" aunt. One aunt he has, *Tanya the Terrible,* and she is ninety-seven years old and a regular witch! She lives in one of Farbstein's houses on East Broadway, and the whole neighborhood is afraid of her. But maybe Pincus did have a legitimate reason for staying away from Schimmel's, and he didn't want to say it. Maybe it had nothing to do with me? Maybe he doesn't even know I'm alive when he's telling one of his stories? It's not important.

"Turgenev," Pincus says, lowering one eyebrow, "what was he? A giant with a big nose! Sometimes on his own estate people would mistake him for a *muzhik*. He looked just like an oaf! Clumsy, and so ugly—it's impossible to describe," and then he rocks his shoulders back and forth, expands his sunken chest, contorts his face, and all of a sudden Pincus is no longer a midget, he's a giant with a fat, sullen face—Turgenev himself! Pincus is my enemy, but I have to admit it: he's a better mimic even than Menashe Skulnik! And now he lets the air out of his chest and it shrinks back to nothing. "And Paulina Viardot," he says, "she was even uglier than Turgenev! Thin, without a chest, stooped like a monkey, but she had big, black, burning eyes that could eat you up alive." Pincus keeps his sunken chest relaxed, but he lets his fingers flutter nimbly, and he contorts his face again, and who knows how he does it, but even from here I can see his tiny, myopic eyes begin to swell up and glow feverishly, and it looks like any minute the two sockets that are holding in his eyes will start to sizzle, and his whole face will be scorched. Schimmel sits with his mouth open and both of Schmulka's legs are beginning to shake. And then Pincus drops his hands heavily on his lap, and his eyes lose all of their luster. "Let her be ugly," he says, "but who, who could resist her eyes! Schubert loved her. Liszt loved her. Musset denied it, but he also loved her. Berlioz was ready to die for her. Heine and Chopin too.

Even her own husband, Louis, loved her! So can you blame Turgenev for following her all over Europe? I'm telling you, the world is ruled by ugly women! Was Queen Victoria a beauty? Or Catherine of Russia? A pretty face can hold you for a minute, and no more."

Soon Pincus will tell how Turgenev and the prima donna met. And first he will mock them and abuse them, and they will both seem comical. Schimmel will have to force himself to keep from chuckling. And then Pincus will slowly warm to them, and he will tell how Turgenev stayed at Louis Viardot's estate, and how Paulina cared for Pelegeya, Turgenev's illegitimate child. And by now Schimmel will no longer want to chuckle. And then Pincus will tell about the later years of Turgenev's life. And soon Schimmel will get ready to take out his handkerchief. Pincus himself will cry. He will cry for Turgenev, and for Paulina, and maybe also for Pushkin, and Gogol, and Lermontov, and Peretz, and who knows how many more? And after the whole Cafeteria cries, Pincus will give the signal, and Wolf the wholesaler will take out his balalaika and everybody will clap their hands and sing, *"Tum Balalaika"* or maybe *"Tzibeleena."* And then I know it's time for me to go home.

I look at my watch. It's almost five o'clock. Irving will be waiting for me with his Volkswagen. Pincus is still telling his story, but what can I do? I have to leave. I stand up and walk past Pincus' table. I know, Schimmel will banish me for at least a week, and the whole Cafeteria will boycott me, but I should worry! After all, I'm moving out. I walk towards the door. Even Fishbein glares at me. And just before I walk outside, I hear Pincus' voice begin to tremble. Maybe he's just getting ready to clear his throat. Who knows? Who cares?

Irving is late. His Volkswagen is not outside the house. Could be he had a bad day in Court? Somebody is calling my name. I turn around. It's Tillie. "Oy," she says, holding her hand over her heart, "let me catch my breath. A woman my age shouldn't have to run." The wrinkled fold of skin hanging down from her neck keeps wagging back and forth, and one of her earrings is missing.

"Yankel, did he start yet?"

"Who?"

She knows that for me Pincus' name is taboo, so she says, "The midget, the midget!"

"He started maybe fifteen minutes ago."

"Oy, they'll kill me if I walk in late." She keeps her hand over her heart. "Yankel, tell me, who is he talking about today? Is it that *meshuggina* Gogol again?"

"No. Turgenev."

"Turgenev," she whispers to herself, "Turgenev," and she's ready to rush inside the Cafeteria. I grab her arm.

"Tillie, what happened? Why were you late?"

"Oy, don't ask! Farbstein came around again. And this time he had with him two goons. He called them City marshals. I saw them from my window. Yankel, I took your advice. I didn't let them in. So I had to wait inside until they left. That's why I'm late."

I look at her. "Was Irving with them?"

"Irving? What would your Irving be doing with such gangsters!"

"Did they bother Mendel?"

"Yankel, let me go. I'll miss the story. *Turgenev!*"

"Tillie, answer me."

"I don't know. Let Mendel look out for himself!"

I release her arm and she rushes into the Cafeteria.
I cross the street. Irving's Volkswagen is still not outside
the house. I walk upstairs and stop in front of Mendel's
door. "Mendele," I say. "Mendel the merchant." No answer. This time I knock. "Mendel. It's me, Yankel." I put
my ear near the door, but I don't hear a sound. Where
could Mendel be? He never takes a step from his room.
Even Pincus' stories can't drive him downstairs. Maybe
he went looking for merchandise? "Mendel, Mendel," I
say to myself, and I go up to my room. I take out my
tweed suit from the closet and brush it off with a whisk
broom. I remove the mothballs from every pocket. "Irving
will like it if I wear a suit. After all, he doesn't want
people to say that his own father is a bum." I put on
the wine-colored shirt and the checkered tie that Irving
bought for me himself. Then I put on the suit. "Finkelstein," I say mournfully to the mirror, "what will I do
when I need another suit? You had to go and hang yourself, hah? And over a woman yet! . . . Yankel, stop
talking. By now Irving must be downstairs, positive!" I
take down my valise from the closet. It's all moldy already, but I should worry! I search through my underwear and find three pairs of underpants and two under-
shirts without holes in them. "I will leave the rest for
Farbstein. After all, the father of an Assemblyman can't
go around with his behind sticking out. It would be a
scandal!" Then I put my scrapbook inside the valise,
and also my ivory chess set—thirty years ago me and
Pincus played chess day and night—and a book of

Sholem Aleichem's stories. I look around the room. And I don't have to stand in front of the mirror to see the wicked smile on my face. Sure, I want to break the lamps, stuff the faucets with toilet paper, mark up the walls, shatter the mirrors. I'm ready to get to work, but then I figure to myself: "Yankel, you will only make trouble for Irving." Don't worry, I will find some other way to take care of Farbstein. I scatter my old underwear all over the room and then I pick up the valise and leave. I walk down one flight. This time I hear a noise coming from Mendel's door. No light comes through the crack under the door. What, is there a robber inside Mendel's room? But what would he have to steal? Mendel's magic samovar? No, it must be Mendel himself. "Mendel," I say, "Mendel the merchant." I hear him. He is crying in the dark. "Mendel, it's me, Yankel. Open up . . . Mendel, I want to buy your samovar." Still he doesn't answer. If Mendel refuses business, something terrible must have happened. I hear him mumbling to himself. "Low-life, bastard."

"Mendele. Rasputin's samovar, let me buy it from you."

"Poison I'll sell you. And a rope to hang yourself."

I know right away it has something to do with Irving. But what can I say? "Mendel, this is the way to talk to a friend?"

" 'Mendel,' he tells me, 'Irving will help us.' And what is the help I get from him? A lawyer letter telling me I have two weeks to move out! And Farbstein threatens me and puts the letter under the door." And then he starts crying again.

"Mendel, I swear to you, I first found out about Irving today. Forget about the letter. I'll talk to Irving. Don't worry. Mendel, trust me."

"Better I should trust a snake!"

"Mendel." He doesn't answer me. "Mendel." I wait by the door for a little while and then I walk downstairs. My hand feels numb and I almost drop the valise. Irving's Volkswagen is waiting outside. Irving himself is leaning against the fender and eating a pastrami sandwhich. Some grease from the pastrami drips down on his tie. I drop the valise on the sidewalk. "Irving, I'm not going." His mouth is so packed with pastrami that he can't even talk.

"Let Farbstein bring around some more of his marshals. They will have to throw me down the stairs before I move out."

Irving's eyes are beginning to bulge, and finally he manages to say, "Pop!" He's still holding half of the sandwich in his hand. "Pop."

"A *lawyer letter* you sent to Mendel? Go 'head, now tell me you never sent it. Stooge!"

"Pop," he says, wiping his lips with a crumpled silk handkerchief. "You're making a big story out of nothing. It's just a formality, that's all. Mendel can tear it up in front of Farbstein's face, what do I care? Pop, I'm telling you, it's nothing. Come on, get in the car."

"No."

"Pop, if you want, tomorrow I'll talk to Mendel myself." He picks up my valise. "Pop, it's light like a feather. Over thirty years you live in one place and that's all you take with you when you move out?"

"Whatever I needed, that's what I took. Irving, promise me that nothing bad will happen to Mendel or Tillie. Otherwise I'm not taking a step."

"Pop," he says, holding up his hand like he's ready to make a Boy Scout pledge, "I promise." He puts the valise inside the Volkswagen. "Wait until you see the place I picked out for you. It's right near the Washington Bridge. And there's a Golden Age Center across the street. Strictly for Jewish people."

"A Golden Age Center?"

"You know. For retired people. Pop, you'll have for yourself a regular harem. The director of the Center tells me there are over a hundred widows. And some of them are still plenty *zavtik*."

"Irving, please, leave me alone with your widows! What are you now, a matchmaker?"

"All right," he says, and he opens up the door for me. I never saw such a car. It's like sitting on the floor! Irving starts laughing to himself. "Pop, do me a favor, buy yourself another suit. Who wears suits now with padded shoulders? George Raft used to wear a suit just like that when he was playing in *Scarface*."

'You should live so!' I want to say, but that's not the way to talk to a son. "Irving, George Raft never in his life wore Finkelstein's a suit. This I can guarantee!"

Once Irving starts, he doesn't let up. "And where did you get that shirt? Pop, tell me, you stole it off a gypsy violin player?"

"Irving, you yourself picked out for me the shirt. And also the tie."

He takes one hand off the steering wheel and pokes his

chest with it. "*I* bought you that shirt? It must have been before the War."

"So let it be *before* the War. A shirt is a shirt!"

"Pop, I know you don't like any of the uptown stores. So take a trip down to *Joe and Paul's* and pick out for yourself a whole new outfit. Charge everything to me. Get whatever you want. A cane or a cravat, who cares? Whatever you buy, I'll pay for it."

"Irving, I tell you what you should wear, hah?"

"Pop, don't get angry. I'm only making a suggestion. Wear whatever you want!"

We drive past the Cafeteria. Through Schimmel's unwashed window I can see Wolf the wholesaler playing on his balalaika. Schimmel and Schmulka are clapping their hands. Pincus is drinking a glass of tea. Irving starts whistling a tune to himself. What is he whistling? Is it a Jewish song? No, it's *"La Cucaracha."* We drive along Second Avenue. I can see old Simon wheeling his push-cart. His back is bent over and he is beginning to limp. What is he selling today? A hot knish or a cold glass of borscht? I want to ask Irving to stop, but he will only say, "That peddler, you'll poison yourself. He hasn't even got a license." What does he know about Simon's knishes? Irving turns the steering wheel and now we are driving towards the West Side. Maybe a change will be good for me, who knows? East Side, West Side, it makes such a difference? Wherever you live, you live! I start humming to myself. *"Shpil balalaika, shpil balalai—"* Irving stops whistling. He watches a girl with long black hair and a tremendous behind start to cross the street. "Irving, remember, I want Farbstein to stay away from Mendel."

"What? Sure, sure, Pop. Leave it to me."

I lean my head against the back of the seat. "Irving, wake me up when we get near the Washington Bridge. I always liked to look at bridges." I close my eyes and right away I see Farbstein's ugly face. The Volkswagen starts to rattle and the face disappears. Now I will try to sleep.

2.

—

East
Side,
West
Side

—

And Irving calls this a room yet! Even the cockroaches are ashamed to share it with me. Cockroaches don't like to take advantage of people. Sure, they have feelings too! Only silverfish you will find in my room. Two whole armies of them, and they are battling all the time. In the bathtub. Under the sink. I spray stink bombs and shout, "Bastards, go!" but it doesn't help. The silverfish refuse to disappear. The two armies are busy fighting with each other, so why should they worry about anything else! And if they want, let them stay. What, I have to go over to West End Avenue and sit in front of Irving's television set, when I can stay home and watch the biggest battles! But the silverfish aren't my only guests. In the bathtub sits a water beetle, and there is no

53

way to chase him out. So I figure to myself, if you can't get rid of an enemy, at least make him a friend. And now I call the beetle "Irving," and every time I want to take a bath, he moves over and gives me room. A gentleman, just like Morris! And if only this beetle could play the fiddle or sing songs, I would hang around him all the time. But he sits without saying a word, my philosopher in the bathtub, and who knows what plans he has on his mind? Could be he's a politician or even a poet. Maybe he's planning to take over New York, or else he's writing a sequel to *Evgeny Onegin*. Sure, my beetle is another Pushkin! Who knows, if I brought him over to Schimmel's, the whole Cafeteria would abandon Pincus and swarm around the beetle. *"Nu?"* Schmulka will say, "so when does the beetle start to talk?" "Schmulka," I will answer him, "you know yourself that the best poetry is left unsaid, so why are you complaining?" And Schimmel, for sure, will give the signal, and Schmulka will throw me out of the Cafeteria together with the beetle. And Pincus will be in command again. But don't worry, I will have my revenge on the midget. This I can guarantee! My beetle will make an appearance at Schimmel's, but for the time being I will keep him in the bathtub. Let him have his poetry and his politics and sit in peace. Why should I disturb him? But how long can I be entertained by a beetle who never speaks? So every morning, after I peel a cucumber and swallow a radish, I run over to the Golden Age Center across the street. Already I am a celebrity at the Center. Sure, Irving is running for the Assembly, and they all think that he will turn out to be another Roosevelt. They don't know yet the deal that Irving made with Farbstein. And why should I tell them?

Let them think what they want! And today, as soon as I walk across the street, Mr. Kapel, the director of the Center, stops everything and says, "Yankel is here." And everybody turns around. Believe me, it's better than being on stage. Even before Pincus poisoned my name, I never made such an entrance. Sure, at Schimmel's I'm an outcast, but here I'm the king! Kapel walks over. "Yankel," he says, "yesterday three widows asked about you. Three! Mrs. Susman even canceled her appointment with her broker. 'The hell with General Dynamics,' she told me confidentially. 'The hell with everything, when Yankel the actor is around!' Yankel, she owns seven houses and a parking lot. I would go after her myself, but she likes only poets and actors. Yankel, it's an opportunity that comes only once in a lifetime."

I want to be polite, but I don't like monkey business. Kapel is worse than Irving already. I know for a fact that he is Mrs. Susman's personal marriage broker, and she has offered him two of her houses if he can find for her a husband. And she is particular yet! Let her own a hundred parking lots! The woman weighs over three hundred pounds, and Kapel himself had to build a special seat for her at the Center. Susman's seat. It's wide like a couch, and it has six metal supports, but it still rocks every time she sits down. One of the pinochle players can marry her if they want, Mrs. Susman is not for me! Kapel keeps talking, but I don't even listen to him. Standing in the corner, surrounded by six or seven widows, is a man with dark glasses and a missing ear. My knees begin to shake. Even with his disguise I recognize him right away. Benya the Torch. Fishbein's hatchetman. The cops are looking for him already for over twenty years. How many men did Benya kill? Only God knows! And if one of the tailors or the grocers on the East Side refused to cooperate with Fishie and pay for protection, Benya the Torch went to work, and the grocer or the tailor could kiss his store goodbye. By midnight it would be burned to the ground. Benya was the biggest arsonist in New York. No one could put together a kerosene bomb like Benya the Torch. All the gangsters sought his services. And Fishie had to lend him out at least once every month. And if a bank burned down in San Francisco, or a saloon was bombed somewhere in Kansas, you could bet your life it was the work of Benya. "Benya," I say to myself, "Benya the Torch." If I'm not careful he'll blow up the Center or burn me alive. But what can I do? If I walk out without saying hello, he'll think I'm trying to avoid him, and not even Mrs. Susman's thousands will be able to save me. So I walk over. "Benya," I say. His one good ear perks up, but he doesn't say a word. "Benya, it's me. Yankel the actor. Fishie's a friend." Still no answer. Then he says to the widows, "Excuse me, ladies, for a second," and he pulls me over to the umbrella tree.

"Yankel," he says, "you are a lucky man. Because of old times, I will give you a second chance. But just mention the name Benya again, I will slit you from one ear to the next. This is from me a promise." And under his coat I can see the handle of a knife. A gangster, what can you do? Who knows how many kerosene bombs he has in his pockets! "You know I am laying low for twenty years, and here could be a detective in retirement. Benya is dead. For your sake, Yankel, don't make the same mistake."

So if not Benya, what then should I call him? Let him

give me already a name! But Mr. Kapel saves my life. He calls from across the room. "Schwartz, what is the latest news from Arabian Oil?"

Benya raises his arm and the knife almost drops out of his coat. "Will be a crash," he says. "Sell everything." Then he talks to me again. "Yankel, don't spoil for me the business. What was before forget! Everybody thinks here I'm a broker."

I know right away what is Benya's plan. He is out to trap a widow. Benya the Broker. *Vey iz mir.* I forget for a minute, and I say, "Benya," and then I correct myself. "Schwartz . . ." His hand is already near the knife.

All the pinochle players put down their cards. In comes Mrs. Susman and another widow. Benya hides his knife. Meanwhile Kapel is already dusting Mrs. Susman's seat. A regular stooge! The whole Center is watching Susman, but Yankel is looking at the other widow. All right, she has a few lines on her face, and a vein here and there on her legs, but honest to God, she is still a beauty. Kapel pokes my chest. "Not for you, Yankel. Not for you. A pauper. She hasn't got a dime to her name. Yankel, a widow without a dowry is like a chicken without a head." Then he walks over to Susman. Benya looks a little nervous. "Yankel," he says, "the fat one is for me."

"With my pleasure!"

Susman sees me and Benya and comes over. Kapel trails behind her. The other widow stays by the door. Benya says hello, and is already quoting figures from Arabian Oil, but Susman doesn't even answer him. "Yan- kele," she says, and right away her pasted-on eyelashes are moving up and down. "Yankele." She opens up her pocketbook and takes out a ticket. "Sholem Secunda's new show. Yankele, at the Elsmere in the Bronx. With Leo Fuchs yet! They are having a special preview for my Auxiliary. Yankel, look at the ticket! For Friday night. Who knows, maybe you'll find a friend there sitting in the next seat?" One of her fake eyelashes falls off. Benya breaks in. "Mrs. Susman," he says, "will be the biggest catastrophe. Whatever you have, sell!" Susman cuts him off. "Schwartz," she says, "you see for yourself that I'm busy. Now is not the time for business. Find for yourself a pinochle partner, and later we will talk." She turns her head away for a minute and pastes the eyelash back on. Benya is already giving me signals, and I know that if I don't walk away soon, I will end up with a knife in my back. And who wants to stay and talk with Susman, when there is a widow standing by the door? So I take the cue from Benya, and excuse myself. "Yankele," Susman says, "Yankele, what about Friday night?"

"I will see," I say. "I will see."

The widow is still by the door. I'm a little nervous. After all, I'm not wearing Finkelstein's suit or even my cravat. But I walk over anyway. She smiles. Yankel, I say to myself, what can you do? Wherever you go, you are a hit!

"Yankel Rabinowitz, no?"

She knows yet my name. Wait, give me five, ten minutes, and I'll bring her over to my room. But maybe the beetle won't like it? And who knows if she'll get along with the silverfish? She'll interfere with their tactics. Irving, Irving, even Farbstein would never dare to pick out for me such a room! With silverfish and beetles, who can bring home a guest?

"Yankel Rabinowitz?" she says again.

I look surprised. "Susman told you my name?"

"I knew you before Susman," she says.

What, she knows me from Second Avenue? Impossible! A pretty face Yankel never forgets! "Schimmel you know?" I say. "Or Itzik the Clown?"

No, she says, she knows only me! Her name is Lena Kaufmann, and when her husband was alive, he took her to see all my shows. "Yankel," she says, "I saw you at the National Theatre in *Muttel the Thief*. What a performance! And *Tevyeh the Dairyman*. And *The Grandpa from Brownsville*." All my shows she saw! But I still look surprised. "When," I say, "when?"

"When?" she says, and she looks at the floor. "Maybe twenty years ago."

It was forty years ago, not twenty! But who am I to argue with a widow! Kapel is trying to get my attention. I know already what he will say. "Yankel, you are making the biggest mistake. Yankel, this widow is poison! Without a cent. You'll end up with her in the doghouse. Yankel, marry Susman, and you will live like a king." He keeps motioning to me, but I ignore him. Susman is sitting in her seat. Both of her eyelashes are on the floor. She looks back and forth at Lena and me. Who knows, maybe she will have us both banished from the Center. Sure, whatever she says, Kapel will do. Only Benya looks pleased. Maybe he thinks now Susman belongs to him. 'Benya,' I want to say, 'the prize is yours!' But I have other business on my mind.

"Lena," I say, "I have a scrapbook at home with pictures from all my plays. *Tevyeh, Muttel,* everything! I live only across the street. Come." Right away she agrees.

We walk past the pinochle players, holding hands. Never in my life did I make such an exit. Not even in *Muttel the Thief!* Even from the door I can hear Kapel's curses. I should worry! If he wants, let him sue me.

"Yankel," Lena says, "I know, offstage an actor doesn't like to act. But maybe you could do a scene for me from *Muttel*."

"With pleasure," I say, "with pleasure. Lena, if you want, we will do a scene together. Pick out a part. Rosalie, the banker's daughter. Or Berkowitz, my bodyguard."

"Rosalie," she says, "let me be Rosalie."

"Fine! We will do a scene from the second act." And what happens in the second act? Don't ask! That lowlife, Muttel, while he is seducing Rosalie, he is also cleaning out her jewels and her father's bonds. And for half the act they wrestle on Rosalie's bed. "Lena," I say, "I have all the props we will need. This I can guarantee!"

So what happens? After I lead Lena across the street, I find my grandson Joel standing outside my door. He is carrying a box filled up to the top with *Vote for Irving* buttons. And sticking out of his pocket is a pastrami sandwich. "Pop," he says, "Pop." The boy is only nine years old, but he is already Irving number two! Wait, give him twenty years, and he will be running for the Assembly too!

"Joel," I say, "your father let you come here alone?"

"No," he says, "Irving dropped me off. We have to meet him later. He's making speeches near Fort Tryon Park."

I want to take Lena inside. But what can I do? I can't chase Joel away. So I say, "Joel, you want Irving to win the election positive?—take the campaign buttons across the street and give them out to everybody in the Center. Then sit and play a game of checkers, and wait for me. Joel, is it a deal?"

Nine years old, and he already knows the score! He looks first at Lena, and then he says, "Pop, we have to find Irving."

Lena can see already that it doesn't pay to argue with Joel. "Yankel," she says, "we will play the scene some other time."

"Lena, meet me outside the Center in an hour. Then we will do two scenes, not one!"

"A bargain," she says, and she goes.

"Joel, soon you will quit school altogether and become Irving's campaign manager, hah?"

"Pop," he says, "who has time?" and he grabs my hand and pulls me outside. Half the buttons fall out of the box, but Joel refuses to stop.

When I lived on Second Avenue, Irving would never bring Joel down to see me. Why? Because Selma, his wife, put the embargo on me. Bluebeard she calls me. And Gypsy. She tells Irving all the time: "Can a man who abandons his wife be any good?" And then she adds: "Irving, what did he ever do for you?" She should join up with Pincus. Together they could poison the whole world against me! What does the woman want from me? I ever said a bad word against her? Honest to God, she's ugly like a witch, but that's Irving's affair. He has to stay with her, not me. But don't worry, Irving is no dope. He would never marry such a witch without a reason. Selma's father owns three delicatessens—two in Brownsville and one in Flatbush—and with his help Irving went

through law school. All right, maybe what she says is
not so wrong. It's true, I never helped Irving out. But
can an actor worry about finances? Could I give Irving
what I didn't have? And God forbid, if I go over to West
End Avenue and visit Irving, Selma boycotts me and
runs inside her room, and could be the biggest fire, she
would never come out! And if I want to give Joel a nickel
or a dime, he shakes his head and says, "Pop, it's not
allowed. Mama says now it's too late to give." But after
he makes his little speech, he grabs the money from me
and runs away without even saying goodbye. And now
when Irving needs me, he takes off the embargo, and
sends Joel with campaign buttons.

"Joel," I say, "I know why your father made me move
uptown. So I could canvass votes for him in his district."
Sure, Irving never makes a move unless it comes back
to him a benefit. "Joel, not so fast. I'm not a race horse!"

So we stand on the corner, and Joel stuffs my pockets
with campaign buttons and starts ordering me around.
"Pop, give them out before Irving comes. Hurry!" What,
in my old age I should become a canvasser? And what
can I say? "Vote for Irving. He will be another Roosevelt." Who could tell such a lie! But Joel keeps pulling
my sleeve. "Pop," he says, "Irving will kill me if he finds
me with all the buttons. Help me give them out." Can
I refuse my own grandson? So I stop a woman in the
street. "Mrs.," I say, "take the button, please." If she
were a widow from the Center, it would be an easy job,
but I never saw the woman in my life. And she looks at
me like I'm a regular loon. Who can blame her? I try
again. "Mrs., my Irving is running for the Assembly.
He—"

"Mr.," she says, "walk away from me before I call a cop," and she throws the button on the ground. This already is war.

"Mrs., have a little respect. Throwing private property on the floor, *hah?* Wait, next time instead of a button, I will serve you with a summons. And when Irving catches you in court, you will wish then that you took the button."

Joel pulls my sleeve. "Pop, Pop, don't start up. There are cops all over the place."

"Good," I say, "good." And then I hear the megaphone croak. "Vote for Ir-ving Rab-in-*o*-witz." Joel's little face crumples up. Just like Irving. "Pop," he says, "the buttons. Irving will kill me." So I take the box from Joel and dump all the buttons into the sewer. "Goodbye and good luck!" Now already I'm a professional canvasser! And in a minute Irving comes by in his campaign car. Blumberg, the law student who works in Irving's office, is driving the car. And Irving sits in back like a king. "Blumberg," Irving shouts, "stop the car." A stooge! Even Joel orders Blumberg around. Who do you think drives Joel to school every morning? Blumberg! And who delivers Selma's laundry, and prepares Irving's briefs? Blumberg, of course! Honest to God, an all-around stooge! Right away Joel starts to shout. "Blumberg, you're late!" Even I join in. "Blumberg, this is the way you drive a car?" And you think he answers back? Not a word! Irving has him trained.

He steps out of the car and opens Irving's door. Irving hands him the megaphone. "Announce me," Irving says, and Blumberg shouts into the lip of the megaphone. "Residents of Washington Heights, come and meet your candidate for the Assembly, Irving Rabinowitz!"

"Blumberg," I say, "you have to blow right in my ear?" And he turns the megaphone in the other direction. Meanwhile Irving comes over. "Joel," he says, "you gave out the buttons?"

Joel makes Irving's famous Boy Scout pledge. "Every one, Irving, honest to God."

Then he turns to me. "Pop, did you butter them up at the Center?" He gets from me an empty look. Right away he pulls Joel's ear. "Didn't you give him the message?"

"I forgot," Joel says, "I forgot."

"Irving, you'll turn the boy into another Dumbo. Leave his ear alone. Whatever is the message, give it to me now."

Irving groans and takes out his handkerchief. "How can I win an election when I have idiots working for me! *Idiots!*" Blumberg hides his head behind the megaphone, and Joel stands behind me.

"I told him ten times, tell-Pop-I'm-going-to-speak-at-the-Center-today. And to make sure you go over and let everybody know."

"Irving, it's not a tragedy. Everybody is still there. When you come in, you can announce yourself."

"And what about Susman?" Irving says.

"Susman?" What, if Susman is working for Irving, then I resign. No, better yet, I'll go around canvassing votes for Schlimmerman, Irving's opponent.

Irving reaches for Joel's ear again. "I told him, I told him." Then he slaps his own forehead. "What's the use? *Idiots!* . . . Pop, Mrs. Susman sits on six different committees, and she's the head of a whole auxiliary. The woman controls three thousand votes." Let it be fifty thousand, I still won't take a step near her. "I told Joel to make sure that you're nice to her before I come over. I gave him a list with everything. Next time I'll know."

"Irving, *shah!* You're making a scandal in the street. This is the way for an Assemblyman to behave?"

"Pop," he says, "when you're right you're right," and he fixes the knot on his tie. "Blumberg, announce me again!" And Blumberg shouts into the megaphone. Then we all walk towards the Center.

"Pop," Irving says, "be nice to her. Susman, Susman! Just until the election. Without Susman on my side, Schlimmerman will win for sure. Pop, please. After the election, do what you want."

I want to tell Irving 'No, impossible!,' but I know he will start to groan, so I agree. For Irving I will make the sacrifice.

We come near the Center, me and Irving walking together, and Joel and Blumberg behind. A little army! Lena is waiting outside. I take her to one side for a second, and I say, "Lena, whatever you see now, don't believe. Pay no attention. Later I will explain." Then I walk into the Center with Irving. Kapel comes over right away. He shakes Irving's hand. "Mr. Rabinowitz. Such a guest! A pleasure, a pleasure." The pinochle players put down their cards, and even the checker players look up. Kapel says hello to Joel, and shakes Blumberg's hand. Me he ignores. And then he says, "Ladies and Gentlemen, we have with us here at the Center a distinguished guest. Irving Rabinowitz, your candidate for the Assembly." As soon as Benya hears Irving's name, he starts signaling to me. His hands are shaking. I walk over to him. "Yankel," he says, "if Irving finds out I'm here, I'm finished for good. Wait five minutes and the whole Center will be surrounded with detectives." Already the knife is half-way out. "Yankel, you squealed on me?"

"Benya," I say, and he's so nervous, he doesn't care what I call him. But why should I take a chance? *"Schwartz,* Irving is here for the election. He doesn't even know you're alive. Honest to God."

"Yankel," he says, "if this is a trick, you can expect from me a bomb. Remember." And then he walks away.

Irving is already standing near Susman's seat. He calls me over. "Mrs. Susman," he says, "you know my father, Yankel the actor. He played *Muttel the Thief* for twenty-seven weeks straight." It was twenty, not twenty-seven. "He broke every record on Second Avenue." Can Irving tell a story!

"I know him," Susman says, without a smile. Irving sees Susman's reaction, and his knees start to bend. What can I do? I promised Irving, so I say, "Mrs. Susman, the Elsmere Theatre. You still have a ticket for Friday night?" And right away Susman's eyelashes start going up and down, and this time she holds her hands in her lap, just in case the eyelashes should fall off. "Yankel," she says, and she gives me the ticket. "My whole Auxiliary will be there."

And, for the first time, Irving smiles. He even puts his arm around me. Tell me, what wouldn't he do for Susman's sake. Now even Kapel shakes my hand. "Yankel," he whispers in my ear, "keep it up, keep it up. You will soon be in the driver's seat. Seven houses, Yankel." He shows me with his fingers. "Seven." Lena is standing near the door. She pretends that she's watching the pinochle players, but I can tell, she is looking at me all the time. I want to walk over, but Kapel is holding my arm. Benya is standing behind the umbrella tree. He sees Susman and me talking together, and I know he will think that I am trying to steal her away. 'Benya,' I want to say, 'don't believe it. I'm acting only for Irving,' but Kapel is still holding my arm. So what should I do now? If I walk away from Susman, Irving will complain that I lost for him the election, and he will cut me off without a cent. And if I stay, Benya will go into action with his torches and his bombs. Either way I'm in trouble! And Lena is still standing by the door. And now I can see, Irving is ready to make his speeches. Irving clears his throat and starts. "Distinguished Citizens . . ." I know already every word. First he curses Schlimmerman and calls him a warmonger, a strikebreaker, and a stooge. The whole Center boos. "Schlimmerman," one of the checker players shouts, "let him roast!" At any other place Irving would also call Schlimmerman "the tool of Wall Street," but he knows about all the stocks and bonds that Susman owns, so he leaves that item out! Then he calls Schlimmerman a draft-dodger, and he tells the Center how his own outfit captured German forts all along the Rhine. Irving doesn't mention that he himself wasn't with his outfit at that time. Sure, while his outfit was capturing the forts, Irving was sitting in a hospital behind the lines with a bad case of piles. But who can blame him? Why should he ruin a good story? And what's the difference if he was with them or not, it was still his outfit, no? Irving tells the story, and everybody listens. Wait, give him time, and he will turn out to be another Pincus! And after the war stories, Irving starts with his favorite topics: Social Security and Medical Care. And right away he uses me for an example. Sure, I have to play the part of Irving's straight man.

Now I'm the one who is the stooge! "And what happens," Irving says, "when an actor wants to retire? Who will look out for him? Who will pay for his medical expenses?" I know the whole story. Soon he will curse Schlimmerman again. So I close my eyes for a second, and call me a loon or whatever you want, but instead of Irving's accusations, I can hear Wolf the wholesaler tuning up his balalaika. What, the whole Center starts to disappear. Honest to God, I'm back at Schimmel's. I'm sitting with Fishie and Morris and Tillie. Even Mendel is there. The whole Cafeteria is waiting for Pincus. Schimmel is boiling potatoes already. Schmulka is standing like a sentry near the door. "Tillie," I say, "you found a place yet?" But she turns her head away. No one will talk to me. Not even Mendel. He sits near Pincus' table and sorts pairs of stockings and drops them into Schimmel's pickle barrel. Wolf tries to entertain the Cafeteria with his balalaika, but no one listens. Soon Schimmel will have a fit. And if Pincus doesn't show up, he will chase everybody out of the Cafeteria. Morris and Tillie are holding hands under the table. Fishbein is drawing crosses and stars on the tablecloth. Schmulka raises his arm and gives the signal. Schimmel brings out the boiled potatoes. Someone comes into the Cafeteria wearing Pincus' Tuesday suit. But today is Thursday, so we know something is wrong. The man who is wearing Pincus' Tuesday suit turns his head towards me. "Farbstein," I say to myself, "Farbstein." Schimmel drops the potatoes. Wolf throws his balalaika. And then, who knows, I can feel someone shaking my arm. "Yankel," Kapel whispers to me. "Your own son is making a speech, and you fall asleep. The whole Center will laugh." I can hear Irving again. He's still busy cursing Schlimmerman. "Schlimmerman says build fallout shelters, but does he worry about your welfare?" "No," the pinochle players shout, "no." Kapel slaps my back. "Another Roosevelt!" Blumberg looks at his watch, and signals to Irving. And Irving signals back, and I know he is getting ready to wind up his speech. "And why does Schlimmerman want fallout shelters?" Irving says with a snarl. "Why? Because he made a deal with the contractors!" Mrs. Susman bangs the armrests of her seat. "Send Schlimmerman to Siberia!"

"To the grave better!" one of the checker players shouts. And Kapel takes Irving's hand and raises it above his head. "A champion! Irving Rabinowitz, the protector of the sick, and the old, and the poor." And the pinochle players and the checker players are ready to start a riot. "Irving, Irving, Irving!" Irving bows and puts his arm around me again. And then we march out of the Center, me and Irving in the middle, and Joel and Blumberg on the sides. Lena is still standing by the door. I whisper to her. "Wait, I'll be back." Benya is still hiding behind the umbrella tree. Susman throws kisses to Irving and me. Kapel rubs his palms together.

Blumberg takes out his notebook. "Irving," he says, "we have to be at City College before three."

I want to ask Irving about Tillie, and Morris, and Mendel, but I can see that he is in a hurry. So I ask him only one question. "Irving, you're still doing business with Farbstein?"

He doesn't even bother to answer the question. "Pop," he says, "three o'clock." And he points to his wrist watch. "I have to make five speeches yet."

Blumberg opens the door of the car. Joel climbs in.

"Blumberg," he says, "you sweated up the whole seat."

"Irving," I say, "Mendel?"

"Pop," he says, "some other time." And he starts giving out orders to Blumberg. "Idiot, start the car. Pop, your place is all right?"

Should I tell him about the battles between the silverfish, or about my guest in the bathtub? "Fine," I say, "fine."

"Pop, promise me you'll cooperate with Susman until after the election."

The motor is running already.

"I promise, I promise."

The car drives off. I can hear Joel shout, "Blumberg, watch out for the traffic lights." I walk back to the Center.

3.

Once upon a Droshky

Every morning, after I pay my respects to the beetle, I promise myself, "Yankel, *today* you will go down to Schimmel's, positive!" But the weeks pass, and I still sit in my room. I send Irving messages. "Irving, you found for Mendel a room?" Sure, campaign buttons he sends me, but he never answers my messages! I wrote Morris twice. "Morris, how is Schimmel? And Fishie? You see Mendel around? Do me a favor, buy from him a cup or a spoon, let it be anything, and I'll send you right away a check from Irving." But even Morris doesn't answer me. And now I worry about Tillie and Mendel, but I still sit in my room. I talk to the mirror and try to comfort myself. "Yankel, you have your pride, no? You're not even welcome at Schimmel's, so why should

71

you run downtown? For what! So you can sit in the corner while the whole Cafeteria worships Pincus? So you can look into Tillie's face, and see your own old age? So Farbstein can threaten you, and Mendel can curse you, and Fishie can refuse you again? Better sit in your room and watch the silverfish! Don't worry, Irving will look after Mendel and Tillie. After all, he promised you, no?" Who can believe it! And still, Yankel sits. But you think I need Schimmel now, when already at the Center there are the biggest intrigues! And who is involved in all of them? Yankel, of course! Lena knows about the pact I made with Irving, so she gave me the green light with Susman! "Yankel," she says, "who wants to interfere with politics?" So every Friday night I go with Susman to the Elsmere or the RKO, and honest to God, it takes an hour before she can fit herself into the seat, and for six rows behind no one can see what's going on. I promised Irving, so what can I do? But there still is another party involved. Benya! If the Torch ever found out that Susman was taking me to the RKO, he would burn me alive in a minute. So I have to be careful. And I tell Susman all the time, "Let it be a secret. No one should know that you take me to the RKO." And to make certain, I say, "Not even *Schwartz* should know!"

And she starts to complain. "What is this, the Secret Service?" But then she tells me, "Yankel, you know I never mix business with pleasure, so why should I tell Schwartz? Whatever I do, this is my affair!"

And now Lena is my accomplice. Sure, she keeps on the lookout for Benya. When the Torch comes around, I stay away from the Center. And then Lena comes over to my room, and right away she takes off her stockings and her girdle, and we both sit on my bed and look through my scrapbook. What can I do with her? She swears on her life that she saw me in *Muttel the Thief,* but when I mention the name Boris Thomashevsky, or Duvie Kessler, or even the great Ben-Ami, she gives me empty looks. And I slap my forehead and say, "Lena, what's true is true. Next to Boris or Jacob Ben-Ami, Yankel Rabinowitz was nothing! And what was *Muttel?* Vaudeville, that's all! What, when Thomashevsky wanted someone to play the Count in Andreyev's play, did he go around looking for Yankel Rabinowitz? No, he found Joseph Bulov, or Ben-Ami, or Sigmund Mogulesko. Believe me, Yankel Rabinowitz he didn't need!"

Then she puts her arms around me and says, "Yankele, let Boris Thomashevsky keep his Count! For me Second Avenue meant Molly Picon, Menashe Skulnik, and Yankel Rabinowitz! And *Muttel* you call vaudeville? You should be ashamed. The scene where Berkowitz, your bodyguard, is shot by the Tepperberg brothers from Brownsville, and you find him already half-dead in back of Saperstein's delicatessen, that was vaudeville? Yankel, be ashamed! My Abie had to borrow extra handkerchiefs for me, that's how much I cried!" And then she makes me put down the scrapbook for a minute, and already her eyeballs are beginning to dance. She calls me 'Muttel,' and what can I do, I call her 'Rosalie,' and we wrestle like *mishegoyim* on my bed! But what does she know, *what!* In 1911, when Yudel Yobelkoff brought over his Yiddish Players from Odessa for an exclusive engagement at the National Theatre, from East Broadway to the Bowery you heard only one name: Yobelkoff! And Yudel also brought with him his own droshky from Odessa, and he would ride through the streets with three or four of his players, and right on top of the droshky they would act out a scene. All the other theatres were ready to close down for the duration. What, how could they compete with Yudel Yobelkoff's company? How old was I then? Ten, twelve, who can remember? But one thing I know. I worked day and night behind my father's dry goods stand on Ludlow Street. Who knew from school! My father was a regular fanatic. On Friday night he would make me board up the stand, and he would run to *shul* and sit for hours with a bowed head, mumbling prayers and twisting the tassels of his prayer shawl. And on Saturday he would repeat the performance. But when it came Saturday night, I opened up the stand for him, and he went back into action. He never had a free moment, my father. He made me sit behind the stand, while he went around robbing merchandise from the other peddlers. And when this didn't satisfy him, he loaded himself up with vodka, and beat me black and blue. And right in front of the stand! Who knows how many times I promised myself that I would set fire to the stand and run away, but where could I go? What could I do? So I took his blows and stayed behind the stand. And one night, while I was walking home from Ludlow Street, I saw the droshky in the middle of East Broadway. The horses were covered with spangles, and the droshky itself was decorated with posters and colored lamps. Maybe a thousand people crowded around the droshky, and the horses kept sneezing all the time. Then Yudel Yobelkoff and two other actors climbed on top of the droshky, and they started to perform. Yudel was wearing a clown's costume, and the other two wore military uniforms. And they sang and they danced, and I stood near the horses and watched. I forgot about my father, and the stand, and everything. The driver rang a little bell and told everybody to come and see Yudel Yobelkoff at the National in Jacob Gordin's play, *Shloime Sharlatan.* Then Yudel acted out a scene from *Shloime,* and no one in the crowd moved or said a word. Even the horses kept quiet. And as soon as Yudel finished his performance, the driver shouted to the horses, and the droshky took off. Yudel stayed on top and danced all the time, and honest to God, wearing his shiny clown's suit in the dark, he was a *dybbuk* or a spook. The lamps kept swaying, and the way the droshky was moving, it looked like it was heading straight for the Valley of the Dead. While everyone else stood around and talked about Yudel and *Shloime Sharlatan,* I followed after the droshky. Half the night I stayed with the droshky, and I saw Yudel perform maybe seven times. I followed him around the whole East Side. And when I came home my father was still waiting for me. His vodka had kept him company. He wanted to throw me down the stairs. But we lived near the Clinton Street precinct, and my father didn't want to take any chances. So instead, he threw me on the floor and punched me and kicked me for over an hour. Who knows how long he would have kept it up, but punching and kicking is strenuous work, no? And he became dizzy from all the vodka, so he sat down for a minute and right away he started to snore. And then, in the morning, he chased me out of bed, and he made me run down and open up the stand. I was practically a cripple from his kicks, but go and argue with my father! So I sat all morning behind the stand and thought only about one thing: Yudel and his droshky! I could still hear the horses' shoes clomping against the cobblestones on Hester Street, and see Yudel himself dancing on top of the droshky. Customers passed by and thought I was a regular loon. It's a lucky thing for me no one called over my father. But it was lunch time already and my father was too busy chasing after the seamstresses from Gluckman's dress shop on East Broadway to worry about me or the stand. And in the afternoon it became worse. I began to imagine myself riding on top of the droshky with Yudel and his band. And now peddlers came over to the stand and robbed pots and pans, and if Dobridushov the chaleh-maker didn't come over and drive the bandits away, my father's merchandise would have been wiped out long before the sun went down. "Yankele," Dobridushov said, "watch the stand or your father will end up in the poorhouse." This is what I prayed for day and night! "And if there's any more trouble, call for me." So I stayed behind the stand and protected my father's merchandise, and after ten o'clock, I closed the stand, and went looking for the droshky. I walked from one end of the East Side to the other. I even stopped in front of the National Theatre. But I couldn't find Yudel, or the droshky, or even one of Yudel's troupe. Who knows, maybe the droshky broke down? Or Yudel became tired of dancing on the roof, and sent the droshky back to Odessa? Whatever the reason, the droshky never showed up again. And don't think I gave up so fast. For six nights in a row I searched for the droshky. And I paid Shlomke the cripple fifteen cents to ask around for news about the droshky. But even Shlomke failed me. Stories he had plenty. "Yankele," he told me, "the droshky sits in the Clinton Street jail." And when I found out that his story was a bluff, he apologized right away, and said, "Even Shlomke is entitled to a mistake." The next day I paid him another nickel, and he swore on his life that Yupke Schmitzel and his boys stole the droshky and were using it for a traveling whorehouse. I checked the story out with Yupke himself. Another bluff! And it's a lucky thing for Shlomke that he was a cripple, or I would have broken his neck for him. But don't worry, he didn't get any more nickels from me! Day and night I thought about Yudel and the droshky, and I knew now what I wanted to be! And in 1913 I chucked my father and his stand, and I became an extra at the National Theatre. And who could complain? Sure, I lived in a room without a sink, and my mattress was covered with bedbugs and lice, but every night I saw Maurice Schwartz and Nadia Nevoslavskaya, and sometimes, when Thomashevsky was giving one of his productions, or when Ben-Ami was on stage, the whole Adler family would visit the National Theatre—Stella, and Luther, and Julius, and Jacob the Great—and I would stand behind the curtain and watch them. And believe me, there will never be another beauty like Stella Adler! Fifteen years old, and I was already in love with her! And when Fishel, the stage manager at the National, saw me standing behind the curtain, he would throw a chair at me and chase me across the stage. "Loafer, I'll hang you from the ceiling! I mean it!" But ten minutes later he would be hugging me, and sending me off with notes to one of the actresses or chorus girls. And by the time I was nineteen, I was already acting with

Zvi Scooler and Wolf Barzel. What, we were better than the Ritz Brothers, any time! And in 1923 Duvie Pinchuk signed me for *Muttel*. But what does Lena know!

She sees a picture of my Clara in the scrapbook. I turn the page. "Yankel," she says, "a beauty! Was she an actress maybe? Yankel, turn back the page. So, talk! Who was she?"

Go fight with her over a picture! "My wife."

"Yankel, you were married?"

"Lena, you know yourself that Irving is my son. So why do you ask such a question?"

"Yankel," she says, "since when does an actor have to be married to have a son?" Let me tell you, Lena is no dope! But I turn the page again, and now she sees a picture of Pincus and me with Jacob Lerner, the playwright, sitting together in Schimmel's. Oy, the arguments they had! Lerner liked only Maurice Schwartz. "Schwartz," he was always saying, "Schwartz. I write my plays strictly for him." And Pincus right away answered back. "Jake, how can you compare Maurice Schwartz with Ben-Ami? One is an actor, and the other is a clown!" And then Lerner would stand up and shake his giant fist in front of Pincus' pint-sized face. "Maurice Schwartz he calls a clown? Yankel, hold me back, before I knock off his head!" And then, like always, there would be a battle. "Skunk! Bastard! Liar!" And how did it wind up? Schimmel the first would come over with a knife in one hand and a fork in the other and drive Lerner out of the Cafeteria. And Pincus would sit and laugh. "Out, out!" What can you do? Even then he was the king of the Cafeteria! And whatever business he had, he conducted right at his table. When Duvie Pinchuk asked

Pincus to rewrite for him the whole third act of *Muttel the Thief,* the contract was signed in front of the whole Cafeteria. And who do you think was the witness? Schimmel, of course! And when Pincus translated one of Blok's poems for the *Forward,* or adapted one of Andreyev's plays, where do you think he worked? In Schimmel's! First he would finish off a plate of borscht and potatoes, and then he would get to work. And God forbid, if anyone ever tried to disturb him, he would motion right away to Schimmel or Schmulka. Only Yankel was allowed to sit next to him! And when he wanted to relax for a minute he would summon Schmulka for the chessboard, and then the whole Cafeteria would crowd around. Believe me, there were better players in the Cafeteria than Yankel Rabinowitz! But Pincus only liked to play with me. "Yankel," he told me in private, "should I sit and play with Zimmerman? Let him be a champion, he still stinks from horseradish!" And then, after five o'clock, Pincus would open up his court. And what was Pincus' court? Listen, and you'll find out! No one trusted any of the downtown *tzadiks,* and who wanted to start up with lawyers and judges? So everybody took their problems to Pincus! The accused and the accusers came over to Schimmel's, and Pincus laid down the law. Me and Schmulka were the beadles at Pincus' court. If anyone spoke out of turn, or started making threats, Schmulka grabbed one arm and I grabbed the other, and we threw the troublemaker out of the Cafeteria. Once Itzie the shoemaker brought his son Jack, who was Fishbein's lawyer, over to Pincus' court. And don't forget, at that time Fishie was still terrorizing the whole East Side, so Jack crossed his arms and thought he was safe. His father

was suing him for nonsupport, and Jack figured to himself that he would come to the Cafeteria, make a fool
out of Pincus, and ruin the reputation of the court. He
even brought two of Fishbein's goons with him. Honest
to God, one of them was Benya himself, and he was
carrying two kerosene bombs in his pockets. And me and
Schmulka knew that with the goons around, we wouldn't
be able to throw Jack out, even if he insulted Pincus or
slapped his father in the face. What could we do? The
court was facing a crisis! So we sat next to Pincus and
waited. And then Itzie told his story. He works all his
life for his son. He sends him through law school. And now
when he's too old already to work in his shop, that same
son won't even help him out with a dime. Oy, if only the
goons weren't there, we would all shout, "A scandal, a
scandal," but who wanted one of Benya's bombs! So we
all shut up and waited for Pincus to act. "He'll back
down," Morris said. "Never," Schmulka answered him,
and he was ready to hit Morris over the head with a
bottle of ketchup. *"Shah,"* Schimmel said, "the court is
in session!" Pincus stood up. "Jack, you have something
to say for yourself?" Jack's arms were still crossed. He
looked once at the goons. "No," he said, "no. Where
is it written that I have to support him?" And then Pincus
pounded the table with his tiny fists. *"Shitface,"* he
shouted, "it should be written with blood across your
head!" I'm telling you, next to Itzie's Jack, my Irving is
an angel already! "They should take you outside and
allow every father on Delancey Street to piss all over
you!" We wanted to cheer. But what could we do? The
goons were still around. "Where is it written, hah? Some
laws don't have to be written out! A father supports his

son, and the son, whenever he can, helps support the
father!" Then Pincus asked the Cafeteria, "Right?"
"Right!" we shouted, goons or not. But even the goons
agreed! Sure, to them it was a joke, but still they helped
support Pincus' decision. "Forty dollars a week," Pincus
said, "and no chance for an appeal!" Benya put his hands
in his pockets and shouted, "Fifty!" So Pincus said,
"Fifty dollars a week," and that was the final decision.
And Pincus' decisions were always binding. For the rest
of Itzie's life, and he lived another twenty years, Jack
had to pay up the fifty dollars. And God forbid, if Jack
skipped a payment, Fishbein sent over Benya for a re-
minder! And the next day, the fifty dollars always arrived.
Now you know. This was Pincus' court!

Lena sees the clippings that are attached to the last
page of the scrapbook. All the clippings are beginning
to crumble. And tiny flakes of paper already cover half
the page. What can I do? The woman found Pincus'
reviews! "Lena," I say, "this is not for you!" You think
I can stop her off? She reads the reviews!

The veins on her forehead begin to jump. "Yankel,"
she says, "the man is a murderer! What did he do to you!
Muttel he calls a public toilet seat. And he says you
would make a good partner for Karimazov, the dancing
bear. I never saw such an enemy! Yankele, who, who was
Pincus?"

"Lena, you believe me, he was once my only friend!"
What, should I tell her about Shaindele and the Catskills,
and how Pincus spit in my face? Who wants to repeat
such stories! She's ready to tear up all the clippings.
"No," I tell her, "no. Yankel likes to torture himself!"
She kisses me three times and then she closes the scrap-

book. She reminds me that today is Friday. "Susman,"
she says, "Susman." And she helps me put on Finkelstein's suit. Then she puts on her girdle and her stockings,
we run outside, and she finds for me a taxi. "Go," she
tells the driver, and I ride over to the Elsmere Theatre.
Susman is waiting under the marquee. "Susman," I shout,
"pay the driver," and I run out of the cab.

"Yankel," she says, "the whole Auxiliary is waiting
inside."

"Good," I say, "now we will make our entrance!"

Then we walk inside. You should see such a theatre!
It used to be a movie house, and in the lobby, on every
wall, you can find twenty-year-old pictures of Sidney
Greenstreet and Judy Canova. There are holes in the
carpet, and everywhere you walk, you step on lumps of
caramel or popcorn. Souvenirs from the movie house!
Sure, without Susman's Auxiliary, the Elsmere Theatre
would never survive!

Half the seats in the orchestra are empty, but still, Susman walks up and down the aisle. She tells me she's looking for the right seat. What, she thinks she's talking to
Maurie the Meshuggina? She wants the whole Auxiliary
to see her, so she parades up and down. Believe me, it's
all for nothing. As soon as she walked in, everyone knew
she was there. She blocked up the whole aisle, and no
one could get in or get out. Already people are complaining. "Susman, sit down, the show is starting any minute."

"Yankel," she says, "you decide!"

What is there to decide? I motion to the nearest empty
row, and now the battle begins. Susman takes three deep
breaths, and tries to squeeze her behind into the seat.
She fails, but what can you expect? It's only the first try!

She sits for a minute on one of the armrests, and the whole seat begins to shake. She tries again! Here it is, only the second try, and already she's getting desperate. "Yankel," she says, "I'll never make it by myself. Give me a push."

"Susman," I say, *"breathe,"* and after pushing down with one hand and pushing in with the other, I finally fit her whole behind into the seat. Now the show begins. What show? Boris Manishevitz and a few renegade Yiddish actors who were thrown out of the Hebrew Actors' Union rent the theatre for a week and send out announcements that vaudeville is making a comeback at the Elsmere. And who would believe such a story? Only Susman's Auxiliary! If Boris Manishevitz ever brought his troupe to the Anderson Theatre, he wouldn't last for a minute. Schimmel or Schmulka would drive the whole troupe out of the theatre, and banish them from Second Avenue for life. But here, in the Bronx, he calls himself "The Prince," and tells everybody that he was one of the biggest stars on Second Avenue! Sure, in 1933 Duvie Pinchuk hired Manishevitz to play the accordion for a wedding scene in one of Molly Picon's shows, and that was his first and last performance on Second Avenue! But as soon as he walks on stage at the Elsmere, Susman cries, "Prince Manishevitz!" And the whole Auxiliary cheers. What can you do? *Mishegoyim!* One of the stage boys brings out his accordion and he sings *"Oif'n Pripetchik"* as only Prince Manishevitz can sing it! Oy, the man can't even carry a tune! And he has the nerve yet to sing the same song again! Then he sings *"Rozhinkes mit Mandlen,"* and already half the women in the audience are crying. Susman herself has her handkerchief

out. "Prince," she says, "Prince." Seven songs he sings
before they finally let him off the stage. And if not for
all the shouting and the clapping I would have fallen
asleep after the second song. And then Morris Blatt, for
twenty years a stage boy at the Public Theatre, and Olga
Manishevitz, the Prince's wife, announce to the audience
that they will do a scene from *Muttel the Thief,* adapted,
Olga says, especially for the Elsmere by Prince Manishevitz himself. This already is too much! My material
he has to steal? I'm ready to call Olga a whore and run
out of the theatre, but who wants to start up with the
whole Auxiliary? So I stay in my seat and promise myself
that I will find a way to get even with the Prince and his
whole troupe. Morris stands near one end of the stage
and calls, "Rosalie, Rosalie," in his squeaky voice. And
right away Olga runs over to him, screams, "Muttel," and
they start to kiss. And believe me, this is not a stage kiss.
This is the real McCoy! I should know! And now, for
the first time, I'm enjoying the show. Sure, it's a pleasure
to see the Prince cuckolded on stage. And in his own
presentation yet! "Yankel," Susman asks me, "they're
doing a good job?"

"Terrific!"

Morris and Olga keep kissing until intermission time.
Then the curtain goes down, the Prince comes out, and
after he bows six or seven times, he announces that coffee
and cupcakes will be served in the lobby.

Someone behind me says, "Benya," and right away I
hide under my seat. I put my head between my knees
and wait for the bombs. "Yankele," Susman says, "Where
did he disappear?" I raise my head slowly. Sitting in the
next row is Benya Kugelman, the shoemaker-poet. Kugel-

man used to sit in Schimmel's day and night, until Schimmel banished him from the Cafeteria. What happened? One day Kugelman drank a tankful of vodka and kvass, and he ran behind the counter and started throwing fishcakes at Schmulka and Pincus. This was bad enough, but when he pissed inside the special vat that Schimmel used to prepare Pincus' borscht, the whole Cafeteria was outraged. Schmulka said that Kugelman should be tried by Pincus' court, but Schimmel swore that if Kugelman came around again he would close up the Cafeteria. And Schimmel the second kept up his father's vow. So now Kugelman is banished for life. But Schmulka takes pity on him, and whenever Schimmel sits and plays solitaire in his room, he sneaks Kugelman into the Cafeteria and allows him a cup of coffee, or maybe a bagel with lox. If you ask me, Schimmel the second worked out a deal with Schmulka. After all, he hasn't got anything against Kugelman. But he doesn't want to break his father's vow. So officially Kugelman is banished. But me and Fishie believe that Schimmel disappears three or four times a week, so that Kugelman unofficially can come into the Cafeteria. Could be we're wrong. But who knows? With Schimmel and Schmulka, anything is possible!

Kugelman sees me and comes over. We shake hands. He looks at me like I'm a loon. "Yankel," he says, "you haven't heard?"

"What?" I say, "what?"

"Schimmel wants to sell the Cafeteria."

"Kugelman," I say, "please."

He places his hand over his heart. "Yankel, on my life. Pincus retired from the Cafeteria. Schmulka sends him messages every day, but still he doesn't show up.

Wolf thinks that maybe the midget had a stroke. But that's only half the story. Fishie is in jail!"

"Fishie in jail? Kugelman, please, what happened?"

"Who knows? He started up with a landlord, and the landlord cried assault, and now Fishie sits in one of the Raymond Street tombs."

"A landlord?" I say. "Farbstein?"

He nods his head.

"Kugelman," I say, "goodbye."

Susman sees me running out of the theatre.

"Yankel," she says, "bring me back a cupcake, okay?" I don't even answer her.

4.

—

Among
the
Brobdingbergs

—

I know already the story. Farbstein had the whole house dispossessed. Schimmel or Schmulka formed a committee, *positive*, but with Farbstein's connections in City Hall, the committee couldn't do a thing. So Fishie went into action. And what did he do? The man can hardly walk! Maybe he sent a letter to Farbstein? Or maybe he met him in the street and told him to lay low? And Farbstein called in the police. From Farbstein what else can you expect? Let him have the whole Cafeteria locked up, no one would be surprised. So who then is the *real* rat-bastard in this affair? Why should I deny it? Irving, of course! Believe me, if Fishie sits now in jail, blame Irving, not Farbstein! Farbstein doesn't take a step without Irving's approval. And he promised me yet! All right, about Tillie and Morris I'm not so worried. They probably moved their bedding into the Cafeteria. But what will happen to Mendel? Schimmel would never take in his pushcart and all his junk. This is positive! And Irving wants to win elections yet. Let him win better a seat in Hell! I know, I know, a father should curse his own son? So if you want, let them reserve a seat there for me too! But please, not next to Irving!

The doorman hears me mumbling to myself. Maybe he thinks I'm a bum from the street. "Announce me," I say, "I want to see Irving." Irving, I tell him again, Irving Rabinowitz. Oy, is this a *schlemiel!* Apartment 7K. So he buzzes Irving's apartment, and then he picks up his little telephone.

"Tell him Yankel is here!"

"I'm sorry," the doorman says, "Mr. Rabinowitz is not at home."

So I take the telephone away from him, and I shout into the speaker, "Skunk, bastard, I'm coming up!" And then I run towards the stairs. So I'll climb seven flights. I should worry! If I end up in the hospital, I'll send Irving all the bills. "Wait," the doorman cries from the lobby, "please!" Who has time to answer him back? I reach the seventh floor and I'm ready to collapse. But you think I stop? I march right over to Irving's door. I try to be a gentleman, so first I ring. I know already that my ringing will bring no results, but I ring again. And then I knock. "Irving, open up!" I knock three times. "Irving, I'll cause a scandal. I mean it. I'll knock on all the doors. Irving? You'll see. They'll throw you out of West End Avenue altogether!" The door opens right away. Sure, if you want action from Irving, you have to threaten him first! I charge through the half-open door, but who do I find standing in the foyer—Irving? No! Just Joel. He's wearing three campaign buttons and a polo shirt with an emblem attached to one of the pockets. And on the emblem are two words. SCHLIMMERMAN STINKS! With Joel around, how can Irving lose!

"Pop," he says, and already he's smiling like Teveleh the Troublemaker, Schmulka's one-eyed cat. "Pop, what's the commotion?"

"Joel," I say, "no tricks. Where's Irving?"

Joel throws up his hands. "Pop," he says, "Irving's not here."

"Not here, heh?" Irving has seven rooms, and maybe nineteen closets, so if he wants to hide from me, what can I do? "Irving, you hear me, Irving? God forbid, if something bad happens to Mendel or Fishie, I'll black-ball your name on the whole West Side. Irving, honest to God, I'll campaign for Schlimmerman. Irving!" I hear a noise coming from the kitchen. I run over right away. "Irving?" Blumberg is standing near the refrigerator. He's preparing pastrami sandwiches. What is he, a boarder already?

"Blumberg, forget the pastrami and find Irving!"

First he opens up a jar of French's mustard and then he shrugs his left shoulder. "Mr. Rabinowitz," he says, "Irving's downtown with a client."

"Blumberg," I say, "you want mustard all over your face? Make a telephone call and get me Irving."

Blumberg holds the mustard jar with both hands. "The client doesn't have a telephone."

"Blumberg, no more stories. You're not now in court.

If I want doubletalk, I can get plenty from Schmulka. I don't need it from you. Go back to your pastrami already. I'll find Irving myself."

I march into the living room. I almost overturn one of Irving's Israeli candy dishes. Good for him! I'll wreck his whole apartment, if he doesn't come out. "Irving! I'm counting till seven. One. Two. Irving?" A door opens. Selma comes out. She's already hissing. Honest to God, the woman is worse than a witch. She's a regular were-wolf! What can I do? I was always afraid of her. So first I calm down, and then I say, "Selma, Irving's around?" You think she answers me? I ask her again. After all, a werewolf is still part human, no? "Selma, I didn't come to ask anything for myself. Who needs favors! But Selma, he made me a promise. He told me that if I moved uptown, he would take care of Mendel, and Morris, and Tillie. I know Tillie already fifty years, can I go and desert her? And now, because of Irving, my friend Fishie sits in jail." Joel and Blumberg come into the living room. They're both eating pastrami sandwiches. "All right, if Irving doesn't want to talk to me, it's his privilege! Just tell him something for me. Irving knows all the judges and the police chiefs. Tell him to free Fishbein from jail. Selma, for Irving it's an easy job. One, two, three! Selma, you'll tell him?"

She puts her hands on her hips, and now she's ready for action. "Whoremaster," she says, "the gypsy whore-master is here!"

"Selma, call me whatever you want, but tell Irving, please."

Now she uses Blumberg and Joel for witnesses. "Look at him! He comes here in the middle of the night . . ."

"Selma, have a heart, it's not even ten o'clock."

She's wearing a hair net with a whole arsenal of pin-curlers underneath. The pincurlers sit on her head like the broken radio tubes inside the chassis that Schimmel still keeps behind the counter. Not even Pincus could compete with Schimmel's radio. What, when they broadcast one of Roosevelt's speeches, Schimmel would threaten to close up the Cafeteria if anyone belched or dropped a spoon. And now, let Irving win the election and right away they'll call him another Roosevelt. And Selma already will become Mrs. FDR! Oy, I would like to stick a battery in her mouth, and then maybe the pincurlers would light up and electrocute her!

"In the middle of the night," she says again, "like a beggar."

"Selma, I know you don't like me. That's an old story already. Just ask Irving to help Fishie."

"Irving has nothing to do with your gypsy friends. Blumberg, tell him to go."

Blumberg knows that if he opens his mouth I'll strangle him on the spot. So he keeps himself busy eating the pastrami sandwich. Then she turns to Joel. And like a stooge he says, "Pop, no more arguments. You better go."

All right, being around Irving and Selma all the time, what can you expect from him? But still . . . "Joel," I say, "this is the way you talk to a grandfather?"

Selma laughs. "He's shocked yet! Look at all the piety. Yankel Rabinowitz, The Jewish King Lear! Deserted by his own brood. And after having granted them all his treasures. And where's the kingdom you gave out to Irving? Where, *Yankele?*"

Who can answer her when she's on the warpath!"
"Selma, you know I was an actor. So what——"

"An *actor*," she says, "an *actor!*" And every time she
moves her head, the pincurlers jump up and down.
Frankenstein's a daughter, what can you do? "Blumberg,"
she says, "you know the facts. When was the last time
that our *Yankele* was seen in a play?"

Blumberg hides his head behind the pastrami sandwich.

"Blumberg!"

Blumberg drops the sandwich. Both his knees are
shaking. "In 1936."

"Selma," I say, "the midget poisoned my name.
Twenty witnesses I can bring you from Schimmel's.
Tonight, if you want. I'll give you the number. Call the
Cafeteria and ask for Schmulka or Morris or Schimmel
himself."

"And *before* 1936?"

"What, *Tevyeh the Dairyman* wasn't a play? Or
Muttel?"

"Ha!" she says. "Half of Irving's clients come from
Grand Street, or Clinton Street, or East Broadway. No
one even remembers your name!"

"All right, a Jacob Ben-Ami I'll never be! But I acted
with Molly Picon, and Zvi—"

"Molly Picon they remember, not Yankel Rabinowitz!"

"So I wasn't one of the biggest stars, it's such a crime?
Kill me if you want! Believe me, I'm not sorry for the
years I spent on Second Avenue. So Irving's clients don't
remember my name, I should worry! I still enjoyed myself."

"*Sure,*" she says, and the mole on her chin is already

bristling. "Sure, you ran around with your chorus girls, and your lady poets, and your tramps from the *Silver Draidl,* and you left a wife and a son to sit at home."

"Selma," I say, "what happened between me and Clara, this is my affair!"

"It was Irving's affair too! He had to watch when your friends brought you home after a week end with one of your tramps. With rouge in your hair and an empty vodka bottle in your pocket and your fly still half-unbuttoned."

"Selma, please. Blumberg, all right. But in front of Joel?"

"Gypsy! Clara's father should have hired someone before he died to throw you in the street and knock nails through your head. Now you come running to Irving! Your friend can rot in jail!"

"Selma," I say, "Selma." She walks out of the living room. Blumberg and Joel trail behind her. Not even a goodbye! I leave the apartment and stand in the hall. Let the whole world abandon me, I should worry! What can you do? I start to cry. All right, she's a witch, but you think she's wrong? Sure, my father had his seamstresses, and I had my chorus girls! Joel comes out into the hall. I hide my face from him and then I wipe my eyes with my sleeve.

"Pop," he says, "are you sick?"

"No, I'm waiting for the elevator."

"Pop, you want me to give Irving the message?"

"What's the use? Your mother will stop him off!"

He puts his hands in his pockets, and I know already he wants something from me. Why else would he come outside?

"Pop," he says, "I have to make posters for Irving. I

need paper and crayons. You want to make a contribution?"

A swindler, what can you do! I give him all my change. Now he says goodbye! And then he runs inside.

I watch the dial on top of the elevator door light up. I keep pressing buttons, but the elevator stays on the fourteenth floor. All right, I walked up seven flights, so now I can walk down! Clara, I say to myself, Clara.

All the actors were after her! Fogelman from the Public Theatre, Lubotsky from the Irving Place, and Yankel Rabinowitz from the National. But her father would never let her come near any of the theatres. And who wanted to start up with him? Nathanson the publisher, he owned three theatres and two magazines, and he was also the managing editor of the Menorah Press. So Fogelman and Lubotsky backed out. "Yankel," Lubotsky said, "Nathanson wants her to marry a professional, so why should I start up? He'll close up the Irving Place if I take a step near Clara."

"Lubotsky," I said, "if you want something special, you have to be willing to pay the price. Let Nathanson throw me out of the National! I'll start a theatre myself in the Bronx."

"Hoo ha!" Lubotsky said. "Who says Clara will see you? She likes only dentists and doctors. A comedy star she doesn't need!"

"Lubotsky," I said, "when Clara Nathanson stands under the canopy, it won't be with a doctor *or* a dentist. This I can guarantee!"

"A bluff," Nathanson said, and he started to laugh. But he didn't know that already Pincus arranged for Clara to come over to the National to see me in *Muttel the Thief*. Sure, Pincus was the whole Menorah Press! He was the main contributor, and everyone knew that when Nathanson retired, Pincus would become the managing editor. And so, on the sly, he invited Clara to the National. "Pincus," I told him, "if Nathanson finds out, you can kiss the Menorah goodbye. Better I'll meet Clara some other time!"

"Yankel," he said, "for six weeks I'm making the arrangements. Now, thank God, Nathanson will be in Philadelphia for two days, and you want to ruin my plans? Don't worry, Nathanson will never know. And Yankel, suppose he finds out? You think Nathanson rules me? Let him keep the Menorah Press! For me a friend is more important. Yankel, Clara will be in the balcony. Leave it to me!"

Go and argue with Pincus! On Saturday night he sat in Schimmel's and sounded the alarm, and on Sunday afternoon the whole Second Avenue showed up at the National for the matinee. Fishel, the stage manager, borrowed extra folding chairs from seven theatres, and he still had to turn away maybe three hundred people. And they stood outside the National and started a regular riot. "Yankel, Yankel, Yankel!" Schimmel and Schmulka were the ringleaders. I saw them myself. Pincus planned everything. And inside was worse than outside! When I walked out on stage, they clapped, and shouted, and stamped their feet. And they wouldn't let me start the performance until I made a speech and bowed to every section of the theatre. And Clara, all the time, was in the balcony with Pincus. But sitting next to her was Botstein, the dentist. Clara's fiancé. So I sent a message up to Pincus right away. And he met me in my dressing room after the first act.

"Pincus," I said, "all the fanfare is fine. Believe me, I appreciate it. But Botstein I didn't bargain for!"

"Yankel," he said, "I had to bring the *schmendrik* along. Clara doesn't take a step without him. But don't worry, we'll get rid of him later. I already made the arrangements." And then he ran back to the balcony.

And after the third act, the whole first row climbed up on stage, and carried me out of the theatre and over to Schimmel's. And then, everyone from the theatre filed into the Cafeteria. Pincus, and Clara, and Botstein too! And Schimmel already had everything arranged. Schmulka prepared the borscht, the vodka, and the gefilte fish. Wolf was there with his balalaika, the Margaretten Sisters came over from the *Silver Draidl* with their gold-plated harmonicas, and after Schmulka brought out his accordion, Schimmel had a regular band! And they made me stand on a box near the counter and sing all the songs from *Muttel*. And while I was singing, Pincus gave the signal, and Schimmel went into action. He stood behind the counter, mixed together some vodka and borscht in a jug, added a little lemon juice and Coca-Cola, and then handed the jug to Botstein. And Botstein took three sips, and right away he collapsed. Schmulka put down his accordion for a minute, and carried Botstein behind the counter. Then I walked over to Clara's table, and after Pincus gave me an official introduction— "Yankel Rabinowitz, the prince of the National Theatre" —I sat down. And while the Margaretten Sisters played "Roumania" on their gold-plated harmonicas, me and

Clara held hands under the table. And next Sunday, after the matinee, Schmulka drove us up to the Catskills, and we stayed there for a day and a half. Two weeks later we were married. Sure, Schimmel built an altar with a canopy, and while Nathanson was in Long Beach, Pincus cornered a rabbi, and we had the ceremony in the middle of the Cafeteria. And that's when all the trouble started. When Nathanson found out how the whole Cafeteria duped him, he banned all of Pincus' articles and threw him off the Menorah Press. Next he paid seven flunky journalists to invent scandals about me, and Pincus, and Schimmel, and *Muttel the Thief,* but after Pincus denounced Nathanson, the journalists, and their accusations in a three-page article that appeared in the *Forward,* Nathanson fired the flunkies and retracted their statements. He also hired goons to put a boycott around the Cafeteria, but Schmulka and his cousins chased the goons all the way to Mulberry Street. And when Nathanson already became desperate, he disinherited Clara and made Botstein his assistant managing editor. Clara soon found out that the whole production at the National Theatre was a put-up job, and after she read the flunkies' articles in the Menorah Press, she went around calling herself "The Victim." She was ready to run back to her father, but Nathanson died two months after the marriage and left her without a cent. Now she called me "Murderer," but what could she do? Even Botstein wouldn't take her back! And she found out for herself that instead of being a prince, I was only a clown, and we had the biggest battles every night. She threw perfume bottles at me and claimed that I ruined her life. She locked me out of the house for weeks at a time, and then went around telling everybody that I refused to sleep with her. And whenever she put the embargo on me, I ran over to Schimmel's or the *Silver Draidl* and stayed with Tillie or with one of Yupke Schmitzel's *nieces*. But why should I tell a lie? One week after we were married, and I was already tired of her. And I went chasing after the chorus girls. What can you do? That's my nature! And you think I really wanted to marry her? I did it for a bet! But now I can't even remember the battles and the bad times. I only remember the Sunday afternoon that Schmulka drove us up to the Catskills. We picked dandelions and black-eyed Susans, and threw blackberries at Schmulka, made friends with a cow and called her "Schimmel," and while Schmulka stood on guard near the car, we undressed each other and swam in a lake behind an abandoned barn. And now, sometimes when I think about Clara, I can feel a pain near my heart that's barbed not with bitterness, but with regret. Whoremaster, Selma calls me, and how can I answer her back?

The doorman sees me and calls me over. He hands me his little telephone, and then walks away.

"Irving?" I say, and I shout into the speaker. "So now you decide to come out of your hole and talk to me, hah?" I rattle the telephone. "Irving?"

"No, Blumberg . . ."

"Blumberg?" I shout.

"*Shhh,*" he says, through the telephone. "Selma and Joel are in the living room watching television. If they find out I'm talking to you, Irving will have me indicted. Mr. Rabinowitz, I'm on your side! I was at your friend Fishman's arraignment."

"Fishbein," I say, "Fishbein!"

"A trumped-up charge! Fishman didn't have a chance. The magistrate gave him the works! . . . Mr. Rabinowitz, Joel's coming. If Irving asks, where should I say he can find you?"

"At Schimmel's, where else! I'm going down to Second Avenue to bail Fishie out of the tombs and see if I can still save the house."

"Mr. Rabinowitz, you can forget about the house . . . I have to hang up. Goodbye."

"Blumberg," I shout, "come back!" Then I hear a click and I let the telephone drop.

"Bastards!"

I glare at the doorman and walk out.

5.

Mendel

The House is still standing. The windows are boarded, and the entrance is blocked off. A sign sits in front of the entrance.

ON THIS SITE
WILL BE ERECTED
A MODERN
19 STORY
APARTMENT BUILDING
SATISFACTION GUARANTEED
M. FARBSTEIN, AGENT
1221 EAST BROADWAY

Sure, first he'll tear down the house, and then he'll throw up another Empire State Building. I can already see the nineteen stories. The building will block out the whole Second Avenue. Schimmel will have to move the Cafeteria to East Broadway. Mendel's window is boarded like the rest, but I still can't believe that he moved out. "Mendel," I call. "Mendele? Mendel the merchant." Who knows, maybe he barricaded himself in the cellar with all his merchandise? I call out his name again. Then I walk across the street to the Cafeteria. I look through the window. It's like a graveyard, honest to God. The counter is closed, and all the tables near the entrance are empty. I walk inside. Where's Schimmel or Schmulka? Only Schmulka's broken box is standing by the door. I walk to the back of the Cafeteria. Morris sees me. He doesn't even say hello. Schmulka is talking to somebody. Oy, it's Benya! The Torch is downtown! Maybe he found out that I took Susman to the Elsmere? It's already too late to walk out. "Yankel," he says, "come here." Schmulka stares at me for a second and then walks to the front of the Cafeteria. Morris frowns.

"Schwartz," I say, "what are you doing downtown?"

"Yankel," he says, "Schwartz you can forget! Benya is Benya again! What, with Fishie in jail, you think I'm going to stay uptown? Twenty-four hours I'm giving them. If they don't let Fishie out of the tombs by then, I will bomb him out! You have my guarantee."

"Benya, please, leave off with the bombs. I'll get from Irving the money for Fishie's bail."

"Yankel," he says, "mention Irving's name again, and you will leave the Cafeteria in a box. This is also a guarantee. If not for you and Irving, Fishie would be sitting here, not in Raymond Street. Farbstein already I will fix! But Fishie sent me a note. 'Leave Yankel alone!'

So count yourself a lucky man. The note saved for you your life. Maybe tomorrow Fishie will change his mind. So I'm holding a bomb special for you." He puts his hand in his pocket. "Yankel, this is not a joke!"

"Benya, I'll free Fishie from jail. You'll see."

Now Morris joins in. "Low-life," he says, "the whole trouble is because of you." I know now who poisoned Benya against me. But what did I ever do to Morris? "Hand in hand you worked with Irving and Farbstein. Hand in hand. The Three Musketeers! Sure, while you went around telling everybody that Irving would save the house, Irving and Farbstein quietly gave us the business. And when Fishie tried to help out, what was his reward? Farbstein slapped him in jail. And God forbid Fishie should get another blood clot in his leg, and—"

"Morris," I say, "since when is Fishie for you such a friend? One name you had for him. Gangster!"

Morris' shoulders stick out like two points. I can see his knees shaking under the table. "A lie, a lie. Benya, I never said such a thing."

"Morris," Benya says, "from calling names nobody gets sent to jail. But from friends who turn out to be bastards, then comes trouble."

Morris sees that Benya is still on his side, and right away his shoulders relax and his knees stop shaking. He punches the table with his tiny fists. "Sure, he stalls us until it's too late for action, and then he runs out."

"Morris, why should you say such a thing? The same day I left, that's when I found out that Irving and Farbstein were working together. That's why I went to you and Tillie. I wanted—"

"Listen to him," Morris says, "listen to him. Tillie!

She was also in the deal. Benya, look! He pretends yet
that he doesn't know! Yankel, this isn't the National
Theatre. You're already off the stage. Tillie is living with
Farbstein!"

Tillie with Farbstein? Impossible! She hates his guts!
Honest to God, you can't trust a soul. The world must
be turning upside down! "Morris, who would believe
such a story?"

He bangs the table again. "The whole Second Avenue
knows, and he still denies it!"

"Morris, I'll kill you, I mean it!"

"Yankel," Benya says, "one more word and I will finish
you off, note or no note!"

Morris moves his chair next to Benya. "Low-life," he
says. "Like a thief in the night he runs away, and then
he comes back with his threats. Crawl better inside a hole
and die!"

"Walk away," Benya says, "walk away."

What can I do? The Cafeteria wants to dispossess me.
You think they're wrong? I walk past Pincus' table. A
band of flies parades near the ketchup bottle. Schmulka
is sitting on his box.

"Schmulka," I say, "you're against me too? No hello,
no goodbye."

"Yankel, who can afford to get on Benya's bad side?
With him here, the Cafeteria is in danger!"

"Schmulka, it's true? Tillie is living with Farbstein?"

"Yankel, it's not such a mystery. What else can you
expect? She had no place to go. So she took her valise
and moved in with Farbstein. And now she stays away
from the Cafeteria altogether. And why should she come
here? Where's the attraction? Two, three days after you

left, Pincus locked himself up in his room, and not even Schimmel's borscht can bring him out."

"Schmulka, Morris lives now in the Cafeteria?"

"No, he moved uptown somewhere. And he comes here once or twice a week, and you should hear the stories he tells about you! Yankel this, Yankel that! You're lucky to find a soul on Second Avenue who will say hello to you. Yankele, between me and you, I never cared much for Morris. True, he plays the fiddle like a major, but a fiddle doesn't make a man! All right, with one point he says I agree. Yankel, for forty years this is your hangout, and then you disappear!"

"Schmulka, I was ashamed. When I found out that Irving was mixed up with Farbstein, I figured it would be better to stay away. But now with Fishie in jail. . . . Schmulka, you went over to Raymond Street? You brought him maybe a little borscht and a baked potato? He always liked Schimmel's borscht."

"Yankel, how could I go? They wouldn't let me in. You remember when Itzie threw a hammer at his wife, and they locked him up for three weeks. We tried to visit him, and what did they tell us? Only lawyers and relatives are allowed! So what's the use of going to Raymond Street for nothing?"

"And what about bail? Schmulka, business is bad, but Schimmel still has a little cash."

"Yankel, I know, I know. But Schimmel sits in his room, and no one can get him out. Without Pincus, he says, who needs the Cafeteria! And when I try to talk to him, he shouts through the door and tells me to shut up. And every day I run up to Pincus, but he doesn't even answer my knock. 'Pincus,' I tell him, 'have a heart,

Schimmel is on a hunger strike. Already the second week. . . . Who says you have to stay? Come down for a minute. Show your face and then do whatever you want!' But if I stood by his door for a lifetime, you think it would help! Yankele, do something. To you he'll listen."

What, he wants me to be a mediator for the midget? "Schmulka, how can you ask? Already twenty-five years we're the biggest enemies."

"All right, I'll try again tomorrow. Oy, Farbstein put a curse on the Cafeteria. It's his fault, everything. Fishie in jail. Schimmel sits—"

"Schmulka," I say, "what about Mendele?"

"Yankel, don't ask! Even Gogol could never make up such a story! Maybe a week after you left, Farbstein shows up at the house with six City marshals. Morris packs his fiddle and comes down together with Tillie. The marshals stand under Mendele's window and order him to come out. Mendel throws down shoes and pots at Farbstein and all the marshals. I watch everything from across the street. 'Boys,' I say, 'will be trouble.' Me and Wolf walk out of the Cafeteria. The marshals protect their heads and run inside the house. I hear Mendel scream. 'Wolf,' I say, 'quick, get Fishie.' Two marshals bring Mendel downstairs. One marshal stands by Mendel's window and throws down half his merchandise. Suits, hats, samovars. People run over and grab whatever they can find. The other three marshals carry down Mendel's pushcart. Mendel starts screaming, 'Someone, please, save my merchandise.' Fishie comes over. He's limping. 'Farbstein,' he says, 'if you want to stay alive, leave him alone.' Farbstein runs behind the marshals.

'Fishbein,' he says, 'now is not thirty years ago. Keep away from me before I make for you plenty trouble. Fishbein, the law is with me.' Fishie says, 'Farbstein, you'll hear from me again. If not now, then later.' Then he calls over me and Wolf, and we start picking up shoes and hats, and put them inside the pushcart. Farbstein leaves with five marshals. The remaining marshal stands outside the entrance. Now Mendel grabs the handles of his pushcart, and he runs like a *meshuggina* towards Delancey Street. Yankel, you know, the pushcart has a missing wheel, and it starts wobbling back and forth. Pots and everything fall out, and leave behind Mendel a trail. 'Mendel,' I shout, 'come back.' But the only answer I get is the squeaking from the three wheels. Already five weeks he's missing. And every other day Wolf scouts around, but he comes back only with stories. 'Mendel is eating garbage near Delancey Street.' 'Mendel stole a satchel from Bendelson's stand on Orchard Street.' 'Mendel is hiding out near the lot on Chrystie Street.' Stories plenty, but no Mendel!"

"Schmulka," I say, "the midget was in the Cafeteria all the time and he didn't come out with Fishie to help Mendele?"

"Yankel, I told you. Pincus abandoned us! He was already sitting in his room. Yankel, do something. It's an emergency. Wait one more week, and we'll have to close down."

"Schmulka," I say, "first I have to find Mendel."

"Yankele, it's after midnight. Spooks you'll find now in the streets. And black cats."

I leave the Cafeteria. Gershen the Gonef is still sitting inside his newspaper stand. He's sleeping. A nickel and two dimes are on his tray. "Gonef," I say, "wake up. Gershen." Right away he puts his blackened fingers over the tray. "Gershen, maybe you saw Mendel around?"

"Yankel," he says, "please, walk away. You'll kill off all my trade. Business is bad enough. You want people to think that Gershen the Gonef associates himself with a fink and a skunk? Walk away!"

"Gershen," I say.

"Yankel, please. I ever caused for you trouble? Please!"

I walk past the stand. What, when did the Gonef ever look out for anybody except himself? He hides in his little cave. Sure, Gershen never takes a step from the stand! Buber is inside his bakery cleaning out his yeast barrels. I knock on his window and wave to him. He turns his head away and pretends that he doesn't hear my knock. I cross Houston Street. Long rows of cars are moving slowly towards the FDR Drive. I walk up and down Chrystie Street looking behind parked trailer trucks and inside empty lots. There are bums all along the street. A nickel? A dime? I walk over to Eldridge Street. A woman with her blouse open down to her nipples motions to me from inside a gypsy tearoom. I smile, but I don't go inside. I see the old house on Allen Street where I lived with Clara for a few months after her father died. Thank God Farbstein doesn't own this house too, or he would condemn it in a minute, and throw up here another nineteen stories. "A hole," Clara called it, "a hole." Sure, the toilet was always stopped up, and the dumbwaiter never worked, but at least we had a garden on the roof, and I grew cucumbers and radishes for Schmulka. And from the edge of the roof I could see

the sign outside Schimmel's Cafeteria, and the house on
Norfolk Street where Pincus still lives. I cross Orchard
Street without taking a look. Mendel would never hang
out with the other peddlers. I come to Ludlow Street.
Jolly Jay Shoes. Fiegenberg's Pickle Products. Julio's
Spanish American Grocery. No Mendel. I pass the place
where my father had his stand. Now it's a travel agency.
Visit Venezuela. Fly TWA. I walk towards Delancey
Street, looking inside all the hallways. I stand for a minute in front of Barish's delicatessen. Here I saw Yudel
Yobelkoff's droshky for the last time. Yudel was dancing
on top of the droshky, and the roof almost caved in. The
driver drank kvass and banged his tambourine, and the
horses pissed in the street and almost flooded the front of
the delicatessen. The jingles attached to the driver's tambourine glowed in the dark. Yudel's boots answered each
sound of the tambourine. A button fell off his costume
and bounced over the sides of the droshky. Half the
crowd scrambled after the button, but it landed near my
feet. I picked it up and gave it to the driver. Yudel never
noticed. I walk past the Loew's Delancey and come to
Clinton Street. I stare at the stone walls of the Williamsburg Bridge, and then walk back towards Houston Street.
Now, where the Clinton Theatre used to stand, on the
left side of the bridge, is a John's Bargain Store. What
can you do? The Clinton was never a success! Who
needed vaudeville when Maurice Schwartz was at his Art
Theatre, or Ben-Ami was at the Irving Place? But after
Pincus chased me off the stage, I put on a beard and
played Maurie the Meshuggina at the Clinton Street. I
had to work, no? And even Schmulka told me, "Yankel,
you let him drive you over to the Clinton? Better sit in

the Cafeteria and tell jokes!" So I took off the beard and kissed Maurie goodbye! A woman wearing sneakers and a cap without a peak asks me for a dime. Both of her ankles are swollen, and her left sneaker is without a shoelace. I give her the dime and she blesses me in Yiddish and Hungarian. I pass Porasoff's grocery store. The lock is still on the door. The store is abandoned already thirty years, but no one has rented it out. I hear someone shout, "I cash clothes," and the words beat down on my shoulders and chest like blows from a hammer. "I cash clothes." My knees give out for a second and I grip the metal railing outside the grocery store. "Porasoff," I tell myself, "at least for once you served a purpose." And now I can already see the lopsided prow of the pushcart. "I cash clothes." His head is still partly hidden. His jacket is open, and he isn't wearing any shoes. His suspenders lop back and forth near his knees. He comes closer. His hands and face are covered with sores. One of his eyes is already closed, and a whole army of flies swarm over his head. He steers the pushcart with both hands. He sees me and stops. He examines me with his one good eye. "Gentleman," he says, "I carry only the finest merchandise." Inside his pushcart sits a mound of rags, a rotten grapefruit, and a blanket pocked with gigantic holes.

"Gentleman," he says. There's some blood on his lip.

I walk over to him. "Mendele," I say, "you recognize me or not?"

He shows me the grapefruit. "Gentleman, the finest samovar you can find." He tips the grapefruit, slowly bending his wrist. Ants are crawling on his hand. "See," he says, "watch the way it pours."

"Mendele," I say, and with my sleeve I wipe the blood from his lip. My arm is shaking, and the sleeve touches his closed eye. Three or four of the flies settle on his forehead. I chase them away. They swarm noisily over the pushcart.

"Mendele, it's me. Yankel. Yankel the actor." I put the grapefruit on top of the blanket.

"Mendele, please, come back with me."

He smiles. I lead him over to the side of the pushcart. "Mendele," I say, "climb aboard. You're going for a ride." I sit him down between the rags and the blanket. He holds the grapefruit in his lap. Some pus begins to drip from the closed eye. He sings to himself. *"Shein vie di levone . . ."* His head rocks back and forth.

I grip the handles of the pushcart and lean forward. The three battered wheels spin slowly and the pushcart moves. He sits quietly now, his feet dangling over the side.

"Mendele," I say, "no more songs?"

The grapefruit falls out of his lap and rolls across the pushcart. The skin of the grapefruit is already bruised, and now it sits in a corner—an orphan, without a friend. I stop the pushcart and put the grapefruit in Mendel's cupped hand. We start to move again. The pushcart is already a veteran. Who knows how many wars it survived! When Fishbein started squeezing all the merchants and the peddlers, you think he let Mendel and his pushcart get by? Fishie wanted tariff from Mendel for allowing him to peddle his merchandise. And he sent Benya around to collect. Three times! The first time Mendel threw pots at the Torch, ran off with the pushcart, and hid out for a week in one of the lots on Chrystie Street. But what could Mendel do? Could he run over to the

Clinton Street precinct with complaints? The man never had a license! And the second time Benya threw over the pushcart and set fire to half the merchandise. "A warning," Benya said, "a warning." But Mendele still wouldn't pay up. "What for?" he said. "I grow money in the street? I work for every cent! So why should I pay off bastards for nothing. Let them croak! Fishbein with Benya together!" And the third time Benya broke off one of the wheels and beat Mendele black and blue. But Fishie said, "Enough! Benya, it's not worth the trouble. What could we collect from him? *Bubkas!* Let the *mamzeh* go!" And believe me, Mendele was the only peddler on the East Side who never paid out tribute to Fishie and his goons! But he still had to pay a price, no? A crippled pushcart and a punctured eardrum from Benya's blackjack! He starts singing again. Then he looks up and shouts, "I cash clothes." A dog limps out of a cellar and stares at the pushcart. "I cash clothes." The dog starts to bark behind my back. I drive the pushcart faster and faster. He smiles and hugs the grapefruit. We cross Houston Street. A man in a truck calls me, "Pop," and asks me for an apple. And when I don't answer him, he shouts, "Spider," and "Jew." I will him and the truck a seat in Hell, and I drag the pushcart towards Second Avenue.

"Sit," I tell him, and I park the pushcart outside the Cafeteria. Schmulka runs over to the window. "Oy," he says, "I knew right away it was Mendel. I heard those wheels maybe a mile away."

Morris and Benya are still sitting in the back. "Lowlife," Morris calls across the Cafeteria. Benya sneezes. He's playing solitaire. Even from the window I can see

the cards laid out on his table. Schmulka comes outside.
"Oy, what did they do to him, what?" He chases away
the flies. "Bandits!" Mendel offers him the grapefruit.
Schmulka wipes his eyes with the end of his apron. "Yankele, Farbstein will pay. You have my word. Come, I
have some witch hazel inside. Help me lift him."

"Schmulka," I say, "you know Mendele. Crazy now
or not, he won't go inside without the pushcart."

"Yankele," Schmulka says, "a pushcart? I have to tell
you? Schimmel will never allow it! He'll chase us all out.
Yankele, please!"

"Schmulka," I say, "without the pushcart he won't go."

Schmulka rocks his shoulders and claps his hands.
"Oy, Schimmel will skin me alive." He walks around
the pushcart once more. "Come," he says, and we wheel
the pushcart through the door. Right away Morris comes
over. "Mendele?" he says. "Schmulka, look, ants are
running all over his body. You'll make an epidemic in
the Cafeteria. Send him out with the pushcart!"

"Morris," Benya calls from the back of the Cafeteria,
"let the *schlimazel* stay!"

"Benya, who says no? But look at his condition!
Benya?"

"What, what," Benya says, and after arranging his
cards carefully in little bundles, he walks over to the
pushcart. Mendel shows around the grapefruit. "Gentlemen, the finest samovar."

"Benya," Morris says, "look at him, even your blackjack couldn't do such a job!"

"Morris, with jokes you will buy yourself a broken
face."

"Gentlemen," Mendel says, "where could you find such a samovar? And for fifty cents." His suspenders dangle over the side of the pushcart.

"Schmulka," Benya says, "lend me a dollar."

"A dollar?" Schmulka searches through his pockets and finds a crumpled dollar bill.

"Tell Schimmel to charge it to my account," Benya says, and stuffs the dollar bill into Mendel's jacket pocket. "Here, Mendele, keep the change." He takes the grape-fruit and walks back to his table.

And now Morris puts on a show for Schmulka and me. He takes his head and lets it rock back and forth in his hands. "Oy, Mendele, what did they do to you, Mendele?" Then he shakes his tiny fists in front of my face. "Low-life, everything here is your fault. Farbstein? No! Irving? No! You, Yankel, you!"

Who has the heart to answer him? I touch Mendel's knee and then walk towards the counter.

"Japface! Snake! If not for you we could have fixed Farbstein and saved the house. First Fishie. Now Men-dele. All the trouble comes from you."

I sit down near Pincus' table. I watch a cockroach crawl up the side of the counter.

"Schimmel should come out of his room and drive you out of the Cafeteria with sticks and knives."

My fingers touch the ketchup bottle. Benya yawns, deliberates over a card, then abandons all his bundles, and plays with the grapefruit.

"I cash clothes," Mendel cries, "I cash clothes."

6.

Fishie

Go and do business with a "schlump"! You should see such a guard! His fly is partway open. His badge sits crookedly on his chest, and is covered with grime. You want more yet? The wooden butt of his pistol is chipped, and his eyebrows move unevenly. What can I do? I show him the two cards that Schmulka forged for me.

"Yankel Fishbein," I say, "a brother."

He looks suspiciously at the cards. "What about a driver's license?"

"What, who drives a car? Officer," I say, "I have to bring with me a bundle of papers for proof? Wait, I'll make one call to the Commissioner, and then, believe me, I'll get some action."

He hands me a manila envelope, and tells me to empty out my pockets. "Key chain, handkerchief, everything. And leave the package on the table. You can't bring anything downstairs."

Right away I rebel. "Officer," I say, "Schmulka stayed up half the night to prepare for Fishie some borscht with schav, and now you put on the borscht an embargo? Inspect the package yourself. Don't worry, you won't find any bombs inside." I show him the bottle of Schimmel's borscht. "Here."

He refuses to look. "It stays upstairs." Go argue with him! He'll arrest me in a minute, and make me Fishie's roommate! I sign for him a card—oy, I almost write *Rabinowitz!*—and after he punches the card three times, he raises his chin an inch and points to the door behind his desk. "They'll take care of you downstairs."

"Thanks," I tell him, "thanks."

He mumbles something to himself, and slumps his shoulders over the desk. The borscht sits near his elbows.

"Oy," I say to myself, "is this a police department!" I walk down three flights, and stand in front of another guard. This one at least is a *mensch*. It's a pleasure to look at him. Even his badge is polished. He takes my card and tells me to sit down. Then he walks out of the room. I have to pass the time, no? So I play a little game with myself. I take Morris and Gershen the Gonef, stand them against the wall, and give them the third degree. "Boys," I say, "it's too late now for apologies. You're stuck in the tombs for good. Here you can forget about Schimmel's borscht and honey cake. No more blintzes with sour cream. Not even a glass of Schimmel's tea. Gershen, get off the floor. You can beg until you're blue in the face. Believe me, it will do you no good. Morris, don't bother unpacking your fiddle. Here a fiddle doesn't mean a thing. The only music you will hear is when the rats race through the pipes, or when the beetles decide to play tick-tack-toe on your chest. Day and night you will sit in the dark. And once or maybe twice a week the guards will throw under your door some slop from the prison cafeteria, and even the rats will refuse it. And for dessert a slice of celery already three months old. Filled with blisters and ant holes. Chew now on that poison the way you chewed before on Yankel's heart! For you two there will be no pardon or reprieve. Slander, Schimmel always says, is a capital offense. Bastards!" I'm talking already like a *meshuggina*. Yankel, please, get off the stage! A man comes into the room. A shrimp, even shorter than Pincus! First he looks to the left and then he looks to the right. Who knows? Maybe he's a convict! He's wearing a fatigue hat together with a lemon-colored tie. A pink handkerchief sticks out of his pocket. Oy, not even Muttel the Thief walked around wearing such an outfit! Pink handkerchiefs all right, but not with a lemon-colored tie! He sits down next to me. Honest to God, he looks just like a rat. The man doesn't have a chin to his name, and his nose twitches all the time. He talks to me yet! "Mr. Marshmallow," he calls me, and "Lemon Drop." Only in the Raymond Street jail could you find such a loon!

"Lemon Drop," he says, "you belong to the house? You come with the woodwork?"

What does he want from me? "Mr.," I tell him, "I'm here to visit a friend."

"Good," he says, and now he has a new name for me.

Ivanhoe! "I have to watch my step. The whole place is flooded with finks." He rolls up his sleeve, and takes out a packet of photographs. All with naked girls. He displays the photographs on the guard's splintered seat. What can I do? I look!

"Ivanhoe," he says, "take your pick. Spades, chinks, Yids. All sizes, shapes, and variations. And if you want something special, I can locate a jobby with an extra tit! High class. All the rabbis wait on line for her!"

A regular tradesman! "Mr.," I tell him, "you have the wrong customer. Your merchandise is not for me!" What, even Yupke Schmitzel never had such a selection! But who wants to start up with bimbos and *bumekahs* with three tits! Maybe seven times the *Silver Draidl* was raided, and if not for Yupke's dumbwaiter, I would have been caught without my underpants every time, like Simkeh the Schlemiel. And I had to sit in the dumbwaiter shaft with my shoulders squeezed between the walls, and with the rats riding on my toes. Who needs trouble! "I'm sorry."

"No offense," he says, "no offense." He folds the packet, and with one flick of his hand, he drops it inside his sleeve. His name is Lucian, and he tells me that he is a magician on the side. Card tricks, he says, are his specialty. I ask him what he is doing around Raymond Street.

"I'm trying to drum up some trade. I've been out of circulation. They just gave me my walking papers this morning. And I had a hard time too. The shylocks don't like to do business on Saturdays." He winks to me. His nose is still twitching. "Most of my clients have been shopping around for another agent. I'd better ride. The finks are on my trail! Take it slow, Ivanhoe!" And he runs out of the room. A *meshuggina!* All right, Yupke was also a pimp, but he never wore a lemon-colored tie! And most of his girls were reserved special for Fishie and Benya. Sure, before Fishbein broke up his gang, the *Silver Draidl* was his headquarters. Goons from the West Side kept throwing bombs inside the lobby, but Fishie always escaped without a scratch. And don't think Fishie was a small-time operator. All the merchants and peddlers paid him dues, but he still wasn't satisfied. So he went after the actors too! Sure, he warned the Hebrew Actors' Union that unless they paid him half their revenue, Benya would bomb every theatre on the East Side. And believe me, the Union was ready to shell out. Who wanted trouble from Fishie! Even Schimmel was afraid to form a committee. But Pincus said to me, "Yankel, come," and we ran over to the *Silver Draidl*. As soon as we came through the door, Yupke stopped us and gave us a warning. "Yankele," he said, "stay away from his table. He's playing pinochle with the Benziger brothers. Twenty dollars a point!" But Pincus wouldn't listen. "Come," he said, and he dragged me over to Fishie's table. "Fishbein," he said, "are you a Jew or not?" The Torch was standing behind Fishie, and his pistol was already next to Pincus' nose! And you should see such a pistol! It blocked out the midget's whole head. And both Benziger brothers had their hands in their pockets.

Fishie kept looking at his cards. "Yupke," he said, "who is this?"

"Pincus," Yupke said, "Pincus."

"Pincus? Yupke, is he a fifty-cent man? Is this Pincus the peddler who works for all the *gonefs* on Orchard Street?"

"No," Yupke said, *"Pincus,* Pincus the poet."

"The same Pincus who writes articles for the *Forward?* Sit down. Benya, put away the cannon. This is the way to treat a guest? He will think that we're not sociable people." Then he threw down his cards. "Mix deal."

One of the Benzigers started to complain. "Fishie, I have a flush with aces, and you call mix deal? This was supposed to be a friendly game."

"Shut up and deal!" Fishie said, and then he turned his chair towards Pincus. *"Nu,* what's the complaint?"

"Fishbein," Pincus said, "when you take from the peddlers, this I don't mind. Business is business. And if it's not one gangster, it will be another. If things get bad, and the peddlers close down, I can still walk around without underwear. But when you start up with the Yiddish theatre, this already is dangerous. Because if your Benya throws his bombs around, right away all the actors and directors will start to panic and maybe run over to Broadway, and there will be no more Yiddish theatre."

"Don't worry," Benya said, "two, three more years and Broadway will be our territory too!"

"Benya, shut up. I like the way he talks." And he gave Pincus the go-ahead.

"Fishbein, you sit in *shul* every Yom Kippur, no? You buy maybe fifty seats."

"There's a reason," Benya said, "there's a reason for the fifty seats. If Augie Amandello's boys ever surrounded us in the synagogue, would be a massacre. With fifty seats clear we can keep an eye on all the exits."

"All right," Pincus said, "forget the fifty seats! Fishbein, you consider yourself a Jew, no? Kill off the theatre and you will commit the biggest crime. They will call you murderer in all the Yiddish encyclopedias. I will write the articles myself. Fishbein, take away our underwear all you want, but please, don't take away our art! Yankele," he said, "sing now a song from *Muttel*. Show the gangsters what they want to kill off!"

So I stood in front of the table and sang, *"Tzuris, Tzuris,"* from the scene where Muttel takes care of all the bankers and their daughters. Even Benya laughed. Fishbein asked me to sing the song again. Then he told the Benziger brothers, "Boys, put some more pressure on the butchers and the pickle merchants. They will have to make up for the revenue that we will lose from the Actors' Union."

And you think this was the end of the story? Two weeks later there was another raid at the *Silver Draidl*, and this time the dumbwaiter was on the bum, and the cops caught me in a minute. They kept making arrests right and left, and all the time Fishie was sitting behind his table playing blackjack with Garfinkel the gambler and one of the Benzigers. He motioned to the police captain who was standing next to me. "My friend," he said, "this man belongs to my party." And the captain excused himself and released me right away. And now Fishie sits in jail!

"Mr. Fishbein!"

I stand up. I notice a pimple on the guard's nose. He is standing near the window, and his ears begin to glow.

"Your brother," he says, "is waiting." I walk behind him. He leads me into a tiny room, then he steps outside, says, "Ten minutes," and locks the door. The left side of the room is divided into three cubicles with screen doors. All three cubicles are a little lopsided. Fishie is sitting inside the cubicle near the door. He is wearing a brown shirt. The screen hides part of his face. "Yankele," he says, "I knew right away it was you. My brother, he tells me, my brother. Sure, Leo sits in Miami with his hardware stores and his hotels. He doesn't even know I'm alive. And who do you think put him in business? Without me he would have remained all his life a bus boy at Rapoport's or the *Royale*. And I broke open heads for quarters and dimes and sent him to Miami Beach. And now every Purim he sends me a five-dollar bill together with a picture of one of his new hotels. My brother Leo! Yankele, someone forged for you a social security card?—Benya?"

"No, Schmulka."

He stands up and walks around the cubicle. His shoulders bang against the narrow walls. He sits down again. "A box," he says, "a box."

"Fishie," I say, "Benya wanted to come, but we warned him. What, if they ever catch him inside, they'll never let him out. He wanted to bring yet his bombs!"

Fishie presses his face against the screen. Behind the wire mesh his left eye looks hollowed out. Oy, what did they do to him! Like a ghost he sits. 'Fishie,' I want to say, 'what, Dracula is here the boss!' But why should I worry him! "Yankele," he says, "tell Benya to lay low. Better he shouldn't have to know from jails!"

"Schmulka prepared borscht and everything, but the

guard wouldn't let me bring it down. A bastard, what can you do?"

"Yankel," he says, "Mendele's still missing?"

He sits inside a box, and he worries yet about Mendel! I'm telling you, Fishie is the gentleman, not Morris! Who cares how many heads he split open! What, maybe it's all a lie? Maybe he was never even a gangster? With all the *mishegas* that goes around today, everything is possible! "Fishie," I say, "don't worry, Mendel will be all right. I found him last night. Schmulka is taking care of him."

"Yankele, they told you what happened when Farbstein came over with his marshals?"

I nod my head. "Fishie, it's all my fault. Irving said move out, and I listened. Maybe if I stayed, it would have turned out different."

"Yankele, *shah!*" he starts to cough and puts a handkerchief over his face. The whole cubicle rattles. A dungeon, what can you do! Who can see inside? Could be there's blood on his handkerchief. That's all he needs yet —TB! He puts the handkerchief away.

"Fishie, should I call a guard? Maybe—"

"Yankele, listen!" He looks at the floor. "After the marshals brought down Mendele, they sat him on the sidewalk. Yankel, his whole body was shaking. He kept watching the *gonefs* grab his merchandise. And they were ready to kill each other over a dented pot or a shoe with only half a heel. Lunatics! Farbstein encouraged them yet. And Mendele sat on the sidewalk with his head between his knees, and mourned alone for his merchandise. And I remembered how I sent Benya after him to collect pennies. 'Benya,' I said, 'teach the *schnorrer* a lesson. Cripple him and his wagon together!' Yankele, for pennies!" I watch him hunch his shoulders behind the screen door. Oy, I'm ready to tear down the door and take him out of the dungeon. Who cares how many guards they have. Me and Fishie will fight them off! "And you know how Mendele hates me. He spits whenever someone mentions my name. *Me* he blames, not Benya. And he's right! And still, when he sat on the sidewalk, he called out my name. 'Fishie, please, save for me my merchandise. You're now my only friend.' Yankele, who could stand there and listen! Honest to God, if I had Benya with me, we would have handled Farbstein together with his marshals! But Benya was uptown! 'Fishie,' he said. And I could see. He was already a little *meshugga* from watching his merchandise disappear in front of his eyes. 'Fishie, I wished on you cancers, and to make sure the cancers came, I dropped pennies inside the *pushke* that Rabbi Tarigansky keeps for the orphans in Jerusalem. Fishie, I'm sorry for the cancers. You're now my only friend.' And what could I do? I told the *gonefs* to stay away, and I tried to save whatever merchandise was left. Then he ran with his wagon. And Yankele, when I saw him with his crooked back and his skinny legs, and with the wagon in front, I promised myself that Farbstein would pay." He starts coughing again. This time he leaves the handkerchief inside his pocket. His whole forehead is wet. Oy, it's like an icebox here, and Fishie sweats! "Yankele," he says, "you know yourself, in my time I was a bigger bastard yet than Farbstein. I have to tell you? And you only know half the stories, believe me. When Porasoff tried to organize the grocers,

Benya went to work on him with his blackjack, and
Porasoff dropped dead in the middle of his store."

"Fishie," I say, "everyone thought he had a stroke."

"Some stroke! With a dent in his head! But his Mrs.
was afraid to say a word. Beryl, her brother, also had a
grocery, and she didn't want him to get the same business
from Benya. So nobody talked. Benya brought his *pushke*
around to all the grocers, and with the money he collected
I paid for Porasoff's funeral and for a first-class monument—from Bendelberg. The best—and I warned Benya
to be careful next time with the blackjack. But Porasoff
wasn't the only one. Yankele, you remember Gluck, the
tailor from Attorney Street? Gluck refused to make a
contribution to the kitty, so Benya threw a bomb outside
his shop for a warning. He didn't know that Gluck's two
children were playing behind the garbage cans. The girl
lost an eye, and the little boy, Shmirele, lost both legs
and an arm." The business about Porasoff I always sus-
pected, but this already I never knew! He gets up again.
The ceiling looks like it's ready to crash down on his
head. He stands for a minute and then sits down.
"Yankel, shouldn't pass a night when I don't think about
Porasoff, and Mendele, and Gluck's little boy, and who
knows how many more! Farbstein could dispossess a
hundred tenants, and it would still be nothing compared
to all the *tzuris* that I caused. Yankele, whatever happens
to me, I deserve yet double. But Farbstein will never
learn. He's a bastard through and through. I warned him.
'Farbstein,' I said, 'stay off the streets.' And last week
I caught him near Norfolk Street. He was collecting rent.
I knew he would make trouble for me. But Yankele, how

could I let him go without a slap? He was only afraid that
I was going to take from him his collection satchel. He
hugged the satchel and cried, '*Gevalt!*' Who wanted his
rent money! I hit him once over the head—'From Mendele, Schmulka, Yankel, and me!'—and then I walked
back to the Cafeteria. Maybe ten minutes later he showed
up with half the precinct. He had witnesses yet! I threatened to kill him, they said. I kicked him and worked on
him with a blackjack! Yankel, you know yourself, that's
Benya's department! When did you ever see me with a
blackjack? Oy, I wish what they said was true! Then I
would be satisfied!" He sits with his hands on his lap.
His chin touches the screen.

"Fishie," I say, "what happened at the arraignment?
Irving's own assistant tells me it was a put-up job."

"Oy, Yankele! They gave me the business from both
ends! They appoint me a legal aid, and I find out right
away that he's working for the court! Who is he?—
Irving's a friend! Even the guard tells me, 'Mr., you are
up the creek! You can't beat the court!' And who is
running the whole operation?—Your Irving!" Sure,
Irving sticks his nose into everything! 'Fishie,' I want
to tell him, 'don't worry. I will bring Irving over to our
side.' But who could say such a lie! "Yankele, before
Spiegelberg, that stooge from the D.A.'s office, reads off
his charges, he runs over to Irving for a conference. And
you think I didn't hear them talk? Even the magistrate
was listening! 'Give him the business,' Irving said, 'give
him the business!' And Spiegelberg isn't satisfied with
assault and battery, no. Yankele, you should hear the
case he made against me! According to him, I am the
president of the Jewish Mafia, and Schimmel's Cafeteria

is my headquarters. And he names all my bodyguards. Schmulka, Schimmel, and you! And Irving is in the court yet! I can see. When he finishes, the magistrate can't stand even to look at me. And he sets bail. Fifteen hundred dollars for one slap!"

"Fishie, you mean it? Fifteen hundred dollars? Who . . ."

"And no bond, nothing! The bondsman tells me I'm a security risk. He doesn't want to start up with the Jewish Mafia! Yankele, I can't complain. How many times did I fix a court! The seesaw goes up, and then it comes down!"

The guard knocks on the door. "One more minute!"

"Fishie," I say, "everything will be all right. You'll see."

"Yankele, stay away from Farbstein. He will work out for you the same deal. Believe me, Raymond Street is not for you!"

"Fishie," I say, "you'll see. Don't worry about the bail. I'll take you out from the tombs. I promise you. On my life. Fishie, how is your leg?"

He pulls his head away from the screen. "Yankele," he says, "it's not the leg what worries me. Believe it or not, this is the first time I sit inside a jail. Without Schimmel's tea or Schmulka's complaints." The whole cubicle is dark, but the metal buttons on his shirt glow behind the wire mesh. He puts his hand against the screen and ruffles the wire. "Yankele," he says, "Yankele."

I put my hand over his. The wire presses against my palm. "Yankele, tell Benya he shouldn't worry. I will be all right. You know, he was always loyal to me—just like Gunga Din! Don't blame Benya for the bombs and the blackjack. Whatever he did, he did for me. Yankele, tell him I'm all right. Tell him the guards put me in charge of the jail. Tell him I have a regular racket. I smuggle halvah into the tombs. Tell him . . ."

The guard knocks again.

"Fishie. On my life. You'll see."

The guard comes into the room. He stares at me. "I'm sorry." I walk out without looking back. I can feel all three cubicles sitting on my shoulders. The guard locks the door. "I'm sorry, Mr. Fishbein. You can come back on Monday." I walk up to the main floor. "Don't cry, Yankele," I tell myself, "it will do you no good. You can't manufacture hundred-dollar bills with tears. And this is what Fishie needs!" Oy, if you only saw the way he sits inside that dungeon, then you would know! Let them throw me better inside the tombs! I'm already a veteran! Sure, I once sat in jail too! What, how long do you think Muttel the Thief went around robbing from the bankers their daughters and their bonds? The bankers banded together and threw Muttele in jail. So they built for me a cardboard cell at the National, and for the whole third act I sat on stage inside the cell. And I screamed, and I moaned. And the whole theatre shouted, "Let Muttel go!" And sometimes, when I banged too hard on the cardboard walls, the whole cell collapsed! And the stage boys would have to run over and hold up the walls. What a performance! All the furriers' wives in the first and second rows threw their handkerchiefs on stage and cried, "Muttele, Muttele!" I'm telling you, it was a pleasure to sit in jail! But I still shouted and moaned. "Muttele," I said, "no more bedroom scenes for you. You're stuck here for life!" And the furriers' wives were ready to faint. And then, in comes Shimion, the philosopher, my only friend. Shimion stands outside the cardboard cell and makes his pronouncements. "Muttele, *shah!* So you sit in a cell! It makes such a difference? Inside, outside, we're all in prison!" Now the whole theatre claps, even the furriers' wives. And Shimion and me sing the final duet, and then the curtain goes down at the National, and I climb out of the cardboard cell. And they don't let me walk off the stage until I sing *"Tzuris, Tzuris"* at least five times. And they make Shimion come out and sing too! But let Shimion walk over to Raymond Street and see Fishie sitting behind the screen, and then, believe me, he would sing a different song!

The guard with the grimy badge is sitting on his desk. His fly is still partway open. A *schlump,* what can you do! I sign for him a form and he gives me back all my belongings, including Schimmel's borscht. I carry the bottle over to the telephone booth near the lobby entrance. I close the door of the booth and right away a fan begins to buzz over my head. "Fifteen hundred dollars. Where can I find such a fortune? Susman, she's the only one! Let her sell one of her houses!" So I sit the borscht on my lap, and then I call the Center. And just my luck, Kapel answers the phone. Oy!

"Yankel," I tell him.

"Who? What?"

"Yankel, Yankel the actor."

He keeps quiet a second. Then he says, "Yankel, if you ever show up here again, I will lock all the doors in your face. You left Susman stranded at the Elsmere, hah? Some joke! In front of her whole Auxiliary. An actor she wanted!"

"Kapel, put Susman on the phone. Tell her, tell her Yankel is ready to marry her." What can I do? Fishie comes first!

"Prick," he says, over the phone, "you missed your chance. Susman doesn't need your *dreck*. She picked out for herself a husband."

"What?"

"Croak!" he says, and then he hangs up. The fan keeps buzzing over my head. Prick he calls me, and he's right. I turned out to be Irving's a stooge. Farbstein should put me on his payroll already. And why shouldn't Tillie move in with him? What did she have from me? And now who knows how long Fishie will sit in jail? And what about Mendele? He sits in Schimmel's with his blanket and his broken pushcart. And I told everybody that I would save the house. Leave it to Yankel! What, when I moved out, you think I didn't know what would happen? I knew all the time! I packed my suitcase and left Fishie to fight my battles! Who wanted to be caught in the middle? That's the way I am. As soon as there is trouble, Yankel runs out! Schimmel should hang me from the ceiling. This is what I deserve! Better yet, Schmulka should throw me inside Mendele's pushcart and drive me around the whole East Side. With a sign over my head. Yankel Rabinowitz. First Class Skunk. Banished From Second Avenue For Life.

"Fishie," I tell myself, "wait." It's time to change my tactics! I'll steal, and cheat, and kill, if I have to. Honest to God, I'll become a gangster, but I'll get Fishie out!

Someone knocks on the door of the telephone booth. Oy, it's Lucian, the pimp with the lemon-colored tie! He pulls open the door. "Ivanhoe," he says, "reconsider. I have a chink outside who is ready to take on all comers. Join the battle! I already lined up seven guards." A guard passes. Lucian sticks his head into the booth. "Cover me," he says, "cover me." The cardboard brim of his fatigue hat presses against my chest. I pull the hat down over his nose, pick up Schimmel's borscht, and run out of the telephone booth. Farbstein, the war is on!

7.

▬

To
Each
His
Own

▬

You think he was always such a bastard? That's

what hurts! He used to sit in Schimmel's with the rest
of us. And the way he worshiped Pincus, you would never
believe it! Sure, he wanted to be a playwright, and he
followed the midget around night and day. With the same
little black notebook that he still has today. And he always had his nose inside the notebook. Whatever Pincus
said, Farbstein wrote down! "Schmulka, peel me a potato." And right away it was written in his notebook.
And if Pincus went to the National or the Irving Place
to review one of Thomashevsky's presentations, Farbstein trailed behind him, his notebook in one hand and
an umbrella with a missing spoke in the other. And what
was the umbrella for? To protect Pincus' head from the

rain? Who says no, but believe me, there was also another reason! Benya had his bombs, and Farbstein had
his umbrella! And whenever one of the producers wanted
to start up with Pincus for writing a bad review, Farbstein came over with his umbrella, and he was ready to
take out the producer's eye. And after all the producers
started to complain, Himmelfarb, the owner of the National, told Pincus that Farbstein would have to check his
umbrella at the box office, so Pincus threatened to boycott the theatre, and Himmelfarb had to give in. But if
Ben-Ami was at the National, Pincus would send Farbstein off on an errand somewhere in the middle of the
Bowery. "Yankel," he would say, "honest to God, he's
for me just like a brother, but who can stand to have him
around all the time? He gives me the creeps with his note-
books! And how can I watch Ben-Ami with that umbrella
sitting next to me. I'm telling you, Yankel, the umbrella
is alive!" And believe me, the umbrella wasn't the only
thing. You should see the way Farbstein chased after
Tillie—oy! What, with Farbstein on your trail, you
think it's a joke? And when Schimmel saw the situation,
right away he picked out for Farbstein a name: *Spider!*
Honest to God, Tillie had to stay away from the Cafeteria.
The spider wouldn't leave her alone! And after she refused him for the hundredth time, Farbstein abandoned
his plays and bought his first house. And now he stopped
showing up so often at Schimmel's, and half the time he
left his umbrella at home. And when he came to the
Cafeteria, he still kept his nose inside his notebook, but
now, instead of listening to Pincus' every word, he sat
and figured out his finances. And Schimmel was ready to
toss him out of the Cafeteria. "Who needs financiers!"

But Schimmel didn't even have to bother. After Farbstein bought his second house, he threw out his umbrella and stayed away from the Cafeteria. *"Mazel tov!"* Schmulka said, *"mazel tov!"* But Pincus was a little unhappy. "The man had possibilities. Now we will never know." And while we sat in Schimmel's and helped Pincus conduct his court, Farbstein gobbled up half of East Broadway. And then, just like a spider, he began to branch out, with here a house and there a house, and today he owns the whole East Side. And now he has Tillie too!

His office is on the third floor. I can see him sitting near the window. His back moves up and down. Whose mortgage will he buy up today? Will Benderman, the pickle manufacturer, find out tomorrow that Farbstein owns all of his barrels? Or will Schimmel be his next victim? Only Farbstein knows! He looks out the window for a minute. He's wearing his black suit. I can see the wrinkles already from the ground floor. Believe it or not, it's Finkelstein's a suit! And the master, just before he killed himself, swore on his life that the thread for Farbstein's suit came from a spider's web. Who believed him then? Now I'm not so sure! I walk up to the third floor. "Farbstein, you started up with the wrong person!" After all, I'm a member of the Jewish Mafia, no? Oy, if his receptionist finds out who I am, she'll lock on me all the doors. So I tell her I'm Irving's a messenger, and right away she lets me in. I take with me Schimmel's borscht, and walk into Farbstein's office. His narrow shoulders are bent over his desk. His bald head sits nervously on his neck like a cannon ball that's ready to be launched. And what is he doing? He's writing something in his notebook! One of his shoulders starts to twitch, and he looks up. "Yankel," he says, and right away he locks all his drawers. Sure, Farbstein keeps a fortune inside his desk. And I feel like hitting him over the head with Schimmel's borscht, and running out with all his rent money. But what good will it do? Will I be able to reach Raymond Street and bail Fishie out? Farbstein will sound the alarm, and the whole police department will invade the East Side, and they'll trap me down like a dog. And when they send me in front of the magistrate, Irving will stand next to Farbstein, and he'll be in charge of the whole show. And when I tell him, "Irving, what, you think it's right to railroad your own father?" he'll slap his sides and complain to the judge. "Your honor, I never saw this man before in my life." Sure, leave it to Irving! So what's the use of starting up? And why should I waste Schimmel's borscht!

"Yankel," Farbstein says, and his eyes are already narrowing down to slits. "If it's trouble you want, you came to the right party. Yankel!"

"Farbstein," I say, "for you *Rabinowitz* is good enough." Who knows how to handle such a snake? First I'll try a few threats! Should I mention Benya's name? No, he'll send half the precinct over to the Cafeteria, and even with all his bombs, Benya won't have a chance. So I'll threaten him in another way! "Farbstein," I say, "the whole Second Avenue is up in arms! Kurele the carpenter is going around to all your houses with a petition. You'll see how many tenants will pay you the rent!"

He laughs to himself. "Yankel, I have a hundred law-yer letters in my desk, signed and sealed. No rent, and out they go in the street. Let Kurele eat his petition!"

I move closer to the desk. He covers his head with his hands. And his elbows start to dance. "Yankel," he cries, "hit me all you want. Tonight you'll be a boarder in the tombs! And don't count on Irving for support!"

That's the trouble. Who can count on Irving for anything! "Farbstein," I say, "stop hiding your head like a turtle. You deserve a good knock on the head, believe me, but for me this is no satisfaction. Farbstein, I want Fishie should be out of the tombs by six o'clock. You hear me, Farbstein?"

He drops his elbows on the desk. "Six o'clock, hah? Yankel, when I'm finished with him, the tombs will seem like a vacation!"

He's a maniac, what can you do? So if not with threats, how else can I force him against the wall? With flattery? Oy! "Farbstein, why should you be such a snake? What, you forgot already the Cafeteria? And Pincus?"

"Pincus," he says, "the Norfolk Street philosopher! The man will die without a penny to his name. Like all of you!" All right, Pincus is my enemy, but he's still a member of the Cafeteria, no? "Farbstein, Schmulka wanted to throw you out by your nose, but the midget said no. What, without Pincus, you were a lost soul! Schimmel took you in, and this is how you repay us?"

"Schimmel," he says, "Schimmel. Yankel, tell me, when Ben-Ami wanted borscht, did he run over to Schimmel's, hah? He sat in the *Royale* with all the actors and the directors. Schimmel's was for *shits!* For paupers and peddlers. Like you and Pincus!"

"Pincus you call a peddler? You used to . . ."

"Sure, I used to lick his boots! Why should I deny it?

And I'll tell you more! I used to shuttle back and forth between Second Avenue and Delancey Street for his chestnuts and his salami sandwiches. And send notes for him to all his favorites. Don't worry, Farbstein doesn't forget! He told me about Chekhov, and Andreyev, and Alexey Tolstoy, and every time I showed him a scene or an act, he said, 'Farbstein, you should be a butcher, not a playwright!' But tell me, where was Pincus' plays? The man never wrote a line! He sat in Schimmel's with his peddlers and thumbed his nose at the rest of the world. Yankel, I didn't stay a dummy like you! My houses still stand. Where, Yankel, where are all your theatres? The National, the Irving Place, the Liberty, the Henry Street, where? Muni was smart. He went to Hollywood. He was better off playing gangsters than sticking around with the Yiddish Art Theatre. You know it yourself. And even Schwartz ended up in Hollywood. With Rita Hayworth yet! Only Yankel Rabinowitz stayed on Second Avenue."

"Farbstein," I say, "from you I don't need lectures." And now I stand over him, with my chin ready to dig into his bald head. "Farbstein, I shouldn't have to ask you again! You're not the only one who knows how to make trouble. I want Fishie out of the tombs! You remember what Pincus did to all the phony garlic merchants with his articles in the *Forward*? They had to run to California without a dime. He will do the same to you!"

"Ha!" he says, "when was the last time that pygmy wrote an article? Before the war! The *Forward* yet! Yankel, you want an exposé? Here, I'll give you all the material. I steal from my tenants, and when they start to complain, I whip them and call for Irving!" He laughs to himself. All his rotten teeth show.

"Oy," I say, "how can Tillie live with you? Look who she picked out for a partner—a regular spider!"

He stands up and thrusts his bald head next to my nose. "Yankel, enough!"

"Enough? For you, Farbstein, nothing is enough! Oy, poor Tillie! Farbstein, you had to buy off Yupke's mortgage and close down the *Draidl?* Sure, Tillie would have been better off working for Yupke, than living with you!"

"Yupke," he says, "Yupke." And honest to God, I move away from him two steps. His whole head begins to swell, and it looks like it's filling up with fire. What, Farbstein is turning into a fire bomb in front of my eyes! Oy, I would like to give it to him. 'Farbstein,' I want to say, 'at least with Yupke she could have a little variety! Yupke would let her pick out her own clientele.' But who wants to start up with him? "Farbstein," I say, "sit down."

"Yupke, hah?" He bangs his elbows on the desk. The receptionist runs into the office. "Throw him out," he says, "throw him out."

"Farbstein," I say, "listen to me! You already ruined one man. Because of you and your marshals, Mendele walks around like an idiot."

"He was always an idiot!"

"Farbstein, please. Fishie sits with a swollen leg. Please. He will drop dead in the tombs. I know. Farbstein, if you want, I'll stay away from Second Avenue for life! Build your houses, all you want. But drop the charges, or pay for him part of the bail? Who can go and raise fifteen hundred dollars?"

"Fifteen hundred, hah! I wanted five thousand! I told Irving to speak to the judge. 'No,' he said, 'fifteen hundred is enough!' Let him rot in the tombs with his swollen leg!" He talks to the receptionist and points his crooked finger at me. "Sarah, if he shows up here again, call the police!"

"Farbstein," I say, "one thing I wish. I should only live to spit on your grave!" When did you ever hear Yankel curse? But if there's nothing left, curses have to do!

"Yankel," he says, "when I'm inside the box, your spit won't mean a thing. Now get out!"

I walk out of the office. I can hear the borscht splash inside the bottle. Yankele, so what did you accomplish? You helped Fishie out with your talk? What, even if I sat on the floor and begged him, would it do any good? All right, I should have baptized him with the borscht. So they would throw me inside the tombs. I should worry! I'll sit with Fishie and play pinochle for match-sticks. I walk down two flights. Oy, Tillie is standing on the ground floor. Even with her earrings, and her brace-lets, and her patent leather shoes, I recognize her right away. What an outfit! Farbstein must have raided all the pawn shops and the bargain basements! The woman is wearing a silk dress with a V-shaped neck, and her bras-sière must be made from steel, because both of her *latkehs* stand out like cantaloupes. And you should see the way they bounce when she walks! *Mommenu!* The Marilyn Monroe of East Broadway! Her legs are still a little swollen, but her dark stockings hide all her bumps and veins. And look how the woman paints her face! Even when I was on stage, I never wore so much make-up. Honest to God, if Yupke ever saw her like this, he would have offered her a contract on the spot and made her the queen of the *Silver Draidl!* She starts walking up the steps. I can tell right away something is fishy. One of the cantaloupes bounces higher than the other. This is my Tillie? Who could believe it! Oy, what did Farbstein do to her! Believe me, I liked her better with her *latkehs* and her wrinkles. She sees me standing on the second floor, and first she put her hands over her face, and then she runs down the stairs. Her earrings fall off. "Oy," she cries, "Oy." She runs inside the rest room on the ground floor. Who can keep up with her? I'm carrying Schimmel's borscht. I pick up both earrings and then I knock on the door. "Tillie," I say, "open up." I can hear her crying behind the door. "Tillie—Farbstein? For forty years you avoided the spider. And now you let him catch you! What, you didn't have a better offer? Schmulka wouldn't let you share his room? Why didn't you get in touch with me? Morris knows where I live." Tell me, how can I be angry with her? When I had my fights with Clara, who do you think took me in? She sent her husband—Moskowitz the furrier!—to Canarsie, and I stayed downstairs with Tillie. Like a prince she kept me, honest to God. She gave me Moskowitz's pajamas, together with all his rights and privileges. "Tillie?"

"Yankel," she says, "please. I have to live too. He's good to me, Yankele. He's good to me. What could I do?"

Do? She could drive a nail through his head! Who knows? Maybe she can bring the spider over to our side? Sure, she has two tremendous persuaders. Let her go to work on him with her cantaloupes! It's for a good cause, no? "Tillie," I say, "talk to him, Tillie. You know Fishie is in jail. Tillie, he'll die there . . ."

"Yankel, what can I do? If I mention Fishie's name, he'll throw me out."

"Tillie, *try!* Mendele is already a *meshuggina.* You want yet another casualty?"

She doesn't say a word. What, she's working out a plan? *Nu?*

"Yankele?"

Whatever she wants, I'm ready to agree!

"Yankel, how is the Cafeteria? The midget came back? Gogol let him keep, but how can I live without Turgenev! Yankele, Schimmel took away my chair? I know, Tillie is banished for life! Yankel, can you go out and buy Schimmel's borscht in a store? And who can boil a potato like Schmulka!"

"Tillie," I say, "I have a present for you. From the Cafeteria."

She opens the door an inch. "Oy, a bomb," she says, "a bomb."

"What bomb? Tillie, Schimmel's borscht!"

Now she opens up two inches more. She sees the borscht. "Schimmel," she says, "Schimmel prepared it for me?"

Why should I lie? "Tillie, borscht is borscht! Take it!"

She closes the door. "Yankel, please, go! I can't do anything for you. Why should I worry about gangsters? I have to look out for myself."

"Tillie . . . he'll die. So he's a gangster. Tillie, tell me, who today isn't a gangster! What, when that Frankenstein, Lopke the lumberman, came into Schimmel's with his three cousins and tried to pull off your dress in front of the whole Cafeteria, who helped you out? Then you didn't call him a gangster!"

"Yankel, he's waiting for me. Who wants to look for trouble? Please . . ."

I leave both earrings and the borscht near the door and walk out of the building. Maybe she's right? Why should she start up? Can I buy her silk dresses with patent leather shoes? I can't even afford fifteen cents for a bus! So I walk back to Second Avenue. I pass Bernstein's delicatessen. What, would he give me a knish on credit? Gershen is sitting in front of his stand. Who needs his hellos! "Yankele," he says, "wait!"

"Gonef," I say, "you're talking to me again? What, the sky must be ready to fall!" Sure, Gershen I know how to handle, but when it comes to Farbstein, Yankel is a flop!

"Yankele," he says, and he raises his blackened palms in protest. "Schmulka told me how you found Mendele last night."

"Sure," I say, "*now* it's good for business if people see me talking to you in front of the stand. Gershen, go and take a good shit for yourself!"

He leans against the stand for support. "Yankel, have a heart! You have to talk so loud? How is Fishie? Schmulka was worried. He thought they wouldn't let you in to see him."

"I saw him," I say.

"You brought him the borscht?"

"Gershen," I say, "if you're so concerned about Fishie, maybe you could help him out a little? Donate ten dollars towards his bail."

He runs inside his stand and closes the door. "Yankel," he says, "who has ten dollars to give? And why should I help him out? He and Benya already took plenty from me. Gangsters! Let him sit where he is. We'll all be better off." The Gonef keeps talking, but I turn my back on him, and walk inside the Cafeteria. Schmulka is sitting on his bench. He's staring at the floor.

"Schmulka?" I say.

He looks up right away. "Yankel, it's no use! Schimmel won't come out. I sprayed some DDT under his door. But you think it did any good? I just came back from Norfolk Street. The midget wouldn't let me in. Yankel, I stood out in the hall and pleaded with him. 'Pincus, Schimmel hasn't come out of his little room in two weeks. Make an appearance, please!' The neighbors started to complain and the super chased me out. Wait. The counter stays closed, and I keep tacking the bills to the wall. And what will happen when the creditors come? Where can I hide? Yankel, Farbstein will buy up the Cafeteria, and build here another house. Wait."

"Where's the Torch?"

"Benya? He made two phone calls and walked out. Who needs him here! Now maybe the Cafeteria will be safe for a little while."

"And Morris?"

"Oy. He cursed you for half the morning and then he went uptown. Yankele, what's the story with Fishie?"

"Schmulka, it's bad. Irving railroaded him. For bail the bastards want fifteen hundred dollars!"

Schmulka slaps his face. "Yankele, he's stuck in jail for life. You'll see, they'll ship him out to Sing Sing." He shakes his fist at the door behind the counter. "Schimmel, come out! You hear? Fishie is in trouble. Schimmel, fifteen hundred. Cough up!" Then he says, "Yankele, wait," and he walks behind the counter and knocks on the door with both fists. "Schimmel, come out!"

Mendele is standing in front of the counter. He's loading empty borscht bottles inside his pushcart. The rotten grapefruit sits on the counter. I walk over to him. His left eye is covered with a patch.

"Mendele, what are you doing?"

He raises the patch. The eye is still closed. "I'm counting my merchandise." The bottles bang inside the pushcart.

"Mendele," I say, "what's for sale? No samovars today?"

His back is bent over the pushcart. I can see his shoulderblades sticking out under his worn shirt. He starts mumbling to himself. "Yankel is a bastard. All my merchandise they stole because of him. All my merchandise." He raises the broken handle and wheels the pushcart across the Cafeteria. "All my merchandise." I walk behind him.

"Mendel," I say, "maybe Yankele didn't know. Maybe he thought Irving would help you out."

The prow of the pushcart knocks over a chair. He stops and collects all the salt shakers from the tables around him. He unscrews their dented caps and sprays the salt over the borscht bottles.

"Mendele," I say, "maybe he didn't know."

He climbs over the sides of the pushcart and sits with two bottles on his lap. He sings to himself. "Yankele, Yankele, Yankele." I walk over to the counter. Schmulka is still knocking on Schimmel's door. "Yankel," he says, "you try. Maybe he'll listen. Schimmel, you hear?"

I stand in front of the door. "Schimmel?" I grip the splintered edges of the jambs. "Schimmel, it's up to you.

Without your capital it's a lost cause. Schimmel, if you saw the way Fishie sits, believe me, you would come out in a minute. Schimmel?"

Schmulka slaps his sides. "It's no use! Yankele, only the midget can drive him out of the room. Only the midget!"

"Schmulka, give me a dime. Don't worry, I'll get some action."

"Fishie needs fifteen hundred, and *he* wants a dime!"

"Schmulka!"

He slaps a dime on the counter. "Go, work now a miracle!"

I walk over to the telephone booth near the counter. The door is broken and the top of the booth is missing. The whole Cafeteria knows the story of Schimmel's telephone booth. When a goon from one of the uptown gangs tried to unload on Schimmel fifty barrels of *goyisher* pickles, Fishie trapped him inside the booth and went to work on him. And Schimmel never bothered to fix the booth. "A monument," he said, "a monument." I should worry! The telephone still works, no? I sit inside the booth and call Irving. Oy, the seat is ready to collapse! Joel answers the phone. "Pop," he says, "Pop."

"Joel," I say, "put Irving on."

First I hear him mumble, and then he says, "Pop, Irving is busy."

"Joel, tell him *Susman.*" All right, a success I'm not, but Irving already I know how to handle! Right away he picks up the phone. "Pop?"

"Irving, you're in trouble. You won't get a vote from Susman, I mean it." So I'll tell him a lie. What, you think it bothers me? "Irving, whatever I say, Susman will do! Vote for Schlimmerman, that's what I'll tell her. Irving, get Fishie out of jail, or you'll lose the election. If Fishie doesn't come out, you don't go in! Irving, this I can guarantee!" Blackmail, what can you do? With Irving this is the only way!

"Pop," he says, "come over."

"Irving," I say, "remember," and then I hang up. I sit in the booth and wave to Schmulka. He starts mimicking me.

"Schmulka, don't worry. The case is closed. Fishie will be drinking your tea tonight."

Mendele is still sitting inside the pushcart. He balances a borscht bottle on his left knee. "Yankel the Thief," he says, "Yankel the Thief." The bottle begins to topple, and falls off his knee. It rolls over the side of the pushcart and lands near the telephone booth.

"Mendele," Schmulka says, "behave! That's all I need! Broken bottles in the Cafeteria. Behave!"

I lean over and pick up the bottle.

"Yankel the Thief."

"Schmulka," I say, and I can hear my voice begin to waver. "Don't worry, I'll bring Fishie back with me."

I leave the bottle on the broken seat and walk towards the door. Mendele is already balancing another bottle.

8.

—

Fathers
and
Sons

—

Sure, I can shout at him and curse, but how can I
be angry at Irving? If now he's a snake, tell me, whose
fault is it? I created the Frankenstein! And what kind
of example did I set for him? When Clara and me threw
pots and dishes at each other, where was Irving? He sat
under the table and saw everything. "Whore," I called
her, and banged her head against the wall. And Irving
would rock his head and cry, "Papa, Papa." And how
did I answer him? "Irving, wait, you're next!" And I'm
not even counting the times when I was drunk! Then I
would chase him around the room and call him, "Clara's
spy." And God forbid, if I ever caught him, I would
swing him by the legs, and hold him upside down.
"Irving," I would say, "take a good look. This is how

149

the world really is!" And who was Irving's protector?
Clara? No! Pincus. Whenever I got tired of throwing
dishes at Clara, I would take Irving with me, and run
over to the Cafeteria. And if Yupke was in a good mood,
he would rent out one or two of his girls, and Schmulka
and me would chase Schimmel out of his room, and give
the girls a chance to put on their kimonos. And who was
the first to sample their merchandise? Yankel, of course!
And if I found out that one of the girls was a dud, I
would stand near the door and shout, "Boys, it's not
worth the trouble," and the whole Cafeteria would boycott the *Draidl* for a week. And we would curse Yupke
and tell him to keep his bargains for himself. But if the
merchandise was good, Schmulka would take out his
pushke, collect the toll, and start the assembly line. And
where was Irving all the time? I stationed him by the
window and told him to keep on the lookout for cops.
What, why do you think I brought him to the Cafeteria!
And once, after Schmulka and me finished off a gallon
of vodka, I took Irving inside the little room. And one
of the girls hid Irving under her kimono and bounced
him on her belly. And you should hear the way Irving
carried on! "Papa," he cried, "Papa, save me!" And what
did I do? Go, call me a father! I laughed and said,
"Irving, now is the time to learn!" What, the boy wasn't
even seven years old! And then I heard a knock on the
door. Pincus came in carrying Farbstein's umbrella. And
he warned the girl to let Irving go. So she pulled Irving
out from under her kimono, and after cursing Pincus,
Yupke, and me, she ran out of the room and told
Schmulka that she was finished for the day. Half the
Cafeteria was waiting on line, and Schmulka refused to

give back the toll, so the other girl had to work double duty. And you think Pincus was finished? He poked the umbrella in front of my face and said, "Yankel, I'm convening the court!" And believe me, he wasn't joking. At seven o'clock Schimmel closed the counter and locked the door. And Pincus made me stand in front of his table. Like a criminal, what can you do? And you should see the witnesses he called in! Yupke, Clara, and Irving. Sure, Yupke had a good time for himself. He called me a whoremaster, and told the court that all the girls were afraid of me. And then it came Clara's turn. And the stories she told about me! The Cafeteria was ready to sentence me on the spot. And don't think the stories weren't true! But still, a husband has his privileges, no? What, I have to sit around and take her insults! And then she brought Irving over to the table and told him to testify. "Tell them," she said, "tell them what a good father you have!" But at that time Irving wasn't a fink. He refused to tell the court. "Papa," he said, "take me home." And what could Pincus do without Irving for a witness? So he closed the case and gave me a warning. "Yankele," he said, "next time you won't get off so easy." But the Cafeteria wasn't satisfied. They didn't want to let me off. Schmulka gave out spoons to everybody, and they started banging on the tables and the walls. But once Pincus makes a decision, who can change for him his mind? The spoons couldn't do a thing! So I walked out with Irving and Clara, and after Irving went to sleep, I threw a pomegranate at Clara and thanked her for her testimony, and then I went back to the Cafeteria. "Schmulka," I said, "stay out of my way. You're now my enemy for life." And he started to laugh. I played chess with Pincus for half the night, and Wolf serenaded me with his balalaika. And the whole Cafeteria sang songs. "Sport," they called me, "Yankel the Sport." And now, when I brought Irving with me to the Cafeteria, Pincus would tell him stories about Hershel Ostropolier and about the citizens of Chelm. And Irving would sit on his knee, and laugh, and call him, "Uncle, Uncle Pincus." Honest to God, they were just like Edgar Bergen and Charlie McCarthy. Sure, Irving became Pincus' a puppet. What, they had a regular routine! The *nudniks* came all the way over from Rivington Street to watch Pincus and Irving perform. And Schmulka stood near the door and collected dimes. You couldn't come into the Cafeteria without paying first a fee! And here's the story! Pincus puts on a beard and plays the wise man of Chelm, and Schimmel fixes up Irving with a putty nose and a cardboard hat, and right away Irving becomes Hershele Ostropolier. Pincus bounces Irving on his knee, and says, "Hershele, tell me, who's the biggest dope in the Cafeteria?" Irving pulls his putty nose. "Schmulka?" The whole Cafeteria cheers, but Pincus nods "No" with his head. "Schimmel?" Now Schmulka and me stand in front of Schimmel and pretend to poke our fingers in his eye. But Pincus gives another nod, and the whole Cafeteria becomes a little curious, and someone asks: "So who then? Who here is the biggest dope?" And now Irving has a revelation. He slaps his cardboard hat and says, "My father!" And this time Pincus nods "Yes!" So Schmulka runs around like a *meshuggina* and pinches me in the right place, and Schimmel shouts, *"Mazel tov!"* But Irving isn't finished. "Uncle," he says, "if my father is such a dope, why do you like him so much?" And now

Schmulka puts his hand behind his ear and waits for an answer. "Why?" Pincus says, "because with a dope it's always easy to get along!" And already there's a commotion in the Cafeteria. Schimmel and Schmulka stand behind me and start to dance. "Yankele," they say, "Yankele," and Wolf accompanies them on the balalaika. I'm ready to walk out. But wait, they're not finished yet. While Schimmel and Schmulka dance, Pincus spreads apart the folds of his beard, and says, "Hershele, you think Schimmel and Schmulka should get married?" And Irving puts his head under Pincus' arm and says, "Why not? One *schlemiel* deserves another!" All right, this already is a show! Schmulka wants to chase Hershele out of the Cafeteria, but Pincus protects him, and Schimmel says, "*Menschelach,* bring out the borscht!" What, who needed the National, when we had such performances! But what happened? Before Irving was nine, he was already taller than Pincus. And now, when he sat on Pincus' knee with the cardboard hat and the putty nose, he blocked out Pincus altogether! And the midget couldn't even deliver his lines. But that was nothing. Believe me, there was more trouble. Clara started complaining that I kept Irving out too late, and once, when Ben-Ami came over to visit the Cafeteria after playing *Shloimele* at the National, Pincus and Irving put on a midnight show, and the performance didn't end until five o'clock. So Clara called in the police. But you think there were any arrests? What, the cops themselves watched the show! And Pincus was so busy preparing all his routines, that he stopped writing reviews and closed down the court, and Irving didn't even bother going to school. Who had the time? "What?" Pincus said, "who needs public school! Hershele is more important! Let him have his education here in the Cafeteria! Can he learn a poem from Pushkin at P.S. 42?" But this already Clara wouldn't stand. She sent the truant officers after Pincus and me. And when they tried to drag Irving out of the Cafeteria, Schmulka ran behind the counter and was ready to throw borscht bottles. But Pincus called a truce. "Schmulka," he said, "put away the ammunition." And he let them take Irving. "What's the use?" he said. "If we chase them out today, they'll only come back tomorrow." And the truant officers sent us a warning. If Irving ever stepped inside the Cafeteria again, me and Pincus would spend two weeks in the tombs! So Pincus sat at his table and started to brood. "Such a combination! Yankel, we were better than *Berele* and *Schmerele!* They had to come and break us up?" And Irving cried every night. He wanted only his Uncle Pincus! And Clara swore that if she heard Pincus' name again, she would run out of the house for good. "So who's stopping you? Go," I said, "go!"

The doorman sees me. This time he acts like a gentleman. Irving told him to be nice. Sure, he wants Susman's votes! "Mr. Rabinowitz," the doorman tells me, "your son is waiting for you," and he walks me over to the elevator. Door-to-door service, what can you do? So I ride up to the seventh floor and knock on Irving's door. Joel opens up right away. You think he calls me "Pop," or says hello? I walk inside. The whole tribe is assembled in the living room. Irving, Selma, and Blumberg. And now Joel joins them. "Yankel," I tell myself, "you'll be lucky if you get out alive!" But I still have to play my

part, no? Let the living room be for me a stage! I roll
my eyes and start to growl. I see my face in Selma's mirror, and believe me, even I'm afraid! What, you think
I spent twenty years at the National for nothing! "Irving,"
I say, *"Susman!"* You think it does me any good? Selma
laughs in my face. And Joel's eyes are already glinting
like the two daggers that Moishele Morgenstern carried
with him on stage when he played *Hamlet at Hester
Street*. And Irving? Don't ask! He's wearing his silk bath-
robe, and he keeps winding the sash around his sleeve
like a phylactery. And some scraggly hairs from his
swollen chest show out between the lapels of his robe.
What, this is the same Irving who sat on Pincus' knee?
Who would believe it! I look at Blumberg, and try to get
from him a little support. A shake of the wrist, a wink,
or maybe half a smile. But even Blumberg is against me.
He turns his head away. Good! Now I know where I
stand. I'll fight off the whole tribe! I walk over to Irving.
He starts unwinding the sash. "Irving," I say, "I want
results!"

"Ha!" Selma says. "Blumberg, throw him down the
stairs."

"Susman," I shout, "Susman." That's my only protection! "Irving, I control her votes."

And now, for the first time, Irving looks at me. "Pop,"
he says, "Kapel just called."

"Kapel?" I say, "Kapel?"

And Selma starts with the chorus. "Kapel!"

I can already feel the noose around my neck. I lean
against the padded shoulders of Irving's studio chair.
"Kapel."

"Pop," Irving says, "Susman is marrying her broker."

"Broker?" I say, and my left eyebrow jumps up automatically. "Broker? Who?"

"Someone by the name of Schwartz."

Oy, Benya, Benya! Susman is marrying the Torch. No wonder why he left the Cafeteria in such a hurry. And I thought he was going over to Raymond Street with his bombs. Benya! I sit down.

"Tell him to stand," Selma says, "I'll have to delouse the chair!"

First Tillie with Farbstein. Now Susman and Benya. Who knows? Next I'll find out that Schmulka stole Schimmel's cashbox and is running off to Atlantic City with Dina the Doublecrosser, Yupke's sister-in-law. Who can I trust? Only Mendele! Irving stands in front of the chair. I can see the hair inside his nostrils. A tassel at the end of the sash touches my leg.

"Pop," he says, "you fixed me for good. Every time Susman hears your name, she has a fit. She won't even be here for the election. She's taking the broker to Miami Beach. And who knows what instructions she left for her Auxiliary. Even Kapel can't find out." He slaps his sides and starts to moan. This already is the Irving I know! "Schlimmerman's in!" He walks across the living room, hunching his shoulders. "Pop?"

I bang the armrests of the chair. "Irving, from me don't expect no mercy! If Schlimmerman needs another campaign manager, I'm volunteering for the job. Better a *schlemiel* than a crook who railroads people and fixes courts!"

Irving keeps hunching his shoulders lower and lower. "Crook he calls me, crook!"

"What, you want a better name? Skunk! Bastard! Take your pick. Tell me, what you did to Fishie, this was legal?"

And now he complains to Selma. "You hear him? I'm risking my whole political career with this election, and he's worrying about Fishbein. He belongs in jail, and that's where he's staying. Blumberg, show him the case we're preparing against Fishbein. The D.A. made me his special assistant. Blumberg!"

Blumberg doesn't take a step. "Irving," he says, "Irving."

"Idiot," Irving calls him, and then he turns to me. "Pop, it's in the bag. We're in touch with one of the old West Side gangs. We'll have all the evidence we need in a week." He struts back and forth, with the sash trailing on the floor. "In the bag."

It's probably a bluff, but who can afford to take a chance! "Irving," I say, "don't worry, whatever trouble you make for Fishie, you'll get back double from me. Maybe Schlimmerman would like to hear about your activities. How you work hand in hand with the landlords."

Now Joel joins in. "Irving," he says, "cut off his allowance. Leave him without a cent." A Jap, what can you do? Selma has him trained!

"Irving, I mean it! Me they'll believe."

Irving slaps his sides again. Then he raises his elbows. "Pop," he says, "once and for all. Who's more important, Fishbein or me?"

What, he expects from me a loyalty oath? "Fishbein," I say, "Fishbein!"

Now it's Selma's turn. Let her say what she wants. I'm ready for the venom. "Irving, ship him back to his Cafeteria. You need his insults? Let him burn with his gypsy band! You ever had anything from him? Tell him never to come here again. He stinks up the halls with his rottenness. Irving, he's diseased. A dirty old man. Selfish. Let him board out with one of his whores. Irving, tell him." Leave it to Selma. She knows where to hit. She could burn out your bowels with one of her words! Believe me! "Irving," she says, "tell him. Tell him what a lousy actor he always was. Tell him how Pincus had to threaten the producers to get him all his parts."

"Selma," Irving says, "shut up!"

"Irving," I say, "let her talk. Maybe I'll learn something yet. Pincus threatened the producers, hah? Witch!" I can feel my hands begin to shake. "I never said I was the best actor on Second Avenue. But nobody got for me my parts. Witch! Sure, the producers were afraid of Pincus. Who says no? But I started at the National before Pincus wrote his reviews!"

She mimics me yet. "He *started* at the National! Some start! Irving knows! You were a stinking stage boy and an extra. They stood you in the corner with a spear and let you play Nuchum the Philistine." She starts to hiss. "Pincus!" Oy, she could blind both my eyes with all that poison. "You were his minion. His favorite pet. His *fairy!*"

"Irving," I say, "I'll kill her. How could she say such a thing?" I stare at the mirror. Yankel is crying!

Joel puts his thumbs behind his ears and dances around the chair. "Fairy, fairy, fairy." Blumberg walks out of the room. Irving catches Joel, shakes his shoulders, and sits him on the floor. "Stay there and keep quiet." Then he says, "Pop, come with me." What can I do? I follow

behind him like a lap dog. We walk inside Irving's room.
And if you enter the room, what do you think you'll find
on the wall? A picture of Yankel at the National playing
Muttel the Thief. And it's framed yet! Pincus' fairy she
calls me. Wait! A broom I'll send her for Chanukah!
And I'll tell her to go for a ride! Irving stands behind
his desk. He takes out two cigars and his 14-karat clipper.
"Pop, calm yourself. You know the way she is. She crawls
right under your skin." He hands me one of the cigars.

"Irving, how could she make such a statement?"

"Relax, relax!" He lights both cigars. We sit and smoke.
"Pop," he says, "Pop." The smoke from Irving's cigar
curls over the desk and hides his face for a minute. "Pop."
The smoke begins to clear, and first I see his chin, then
one ear, and both eyes. Like a sphinx he sits.

"Pop, you want to see Schlimmerman win? Help me
out. Pop?"

Sure, the cops work you over with their bright lights
and their clubs, and Irving takes you inside his room and
gives you a cigar. "Pop?"

"Irving," I say, "so what can I do for you?"

"Let Susman marry her broker, but go over and talk
to her. Who knows what you did?—but apologize! At
least you don't have to be an enemy. Pop? You'll talk
to her?"

"And what about Fishie?"

I can hear him slap his sides. "Fishbein again!"

"Irving, you should know! As long as Fishbein sits in
jail, I don't do a thing!"

"Pop, what can I do for him, what?"

"Irving, make out a check for fifteen hundred dollars,

and I'll get Susman to divorce her broker even before they're married. You want her votes? You'll have to pay for it! Fifteen hundred for Fishie's bail!"

"Pop, you know I want to help you out. You think it makes a difference to me if Fishbein stays in jail or not? But what can I do? If I give you the money, and Farbstein finds out, he'll sic all the District Leaders on me. Pop, I'm caught in the middle. Here, I'll pay part of the bail. You know you can always count on me for a pal." He takes two ten dollar bills out of his wallet. "Pop, for the bail!"

"Irving, keep your twenty dollars. With such help Fishie will sit in Raymond Street forever!"

"Pop, so what can I do?" He puts back the twenty dollars, and folds the wallet. "All right, all right. I'll talk to the D.A. I'll get him to go slow on Fishbein. Okay? Simple assault. He'll be out in thirty days. And I'll put some pressure on Farbstein. Don't worry, Fishbein will get his bail."

"Irving, it's a promise? Swear on your life!"

He makes his Boy Scout pledge. "Pop," he says, "you're a tough customer." He sticks both hands inside one of the drawers and pulls out two fistfuls of *Vote for Irving* buttons. "Here," he says, and he packs all my pockets with the buttons. "For the Center. And Pop, with Susman. You know. Put in a good word. And knock Schlimmerman every chance you get. Pop?"

"Irving, stop coaching me! When I'm finished with Schlimmerman, he won't be able to show his face in Washington Heights. But Irving, if Fishie gets the business, believe me, it will be the opposite way around. You'll get the business from me!"

"Pop," he says, "we made an agreement. I'll take care of Fishie. You can count on it!"

"Sure," I say, "sure." Oy! God help Fishie with Irving taking care of him! But what can I do? Irving is already the last resort! We both stand up. Irving puts his arm around my shoulder, and we walk out of the room. Joel and Selma are waiting in the hall. Where's Blumberg? Joel is holding a plastic tommy gun. Honest to God, he wants to shoot me down! And Selma is ready to tear out my eyes! And Fishie they call a gangster! Irving leads me over to the door. "Pop," he says, "relax, relax!" His arm is still around my shoulder. He opens the door for me. I walk out and stand near the elevator. He sticks his head into the hallway. "Pop, don't forget to give out the buttons!"

"Irving," I say, "how could I forget?"

Now he closes the door. Believe me, someone should write a book about fathers and sons! All right, why should Irving love me? What's true is true! Did I love my father? How many times did I pray that all the peddlers would band together and break his neck! I would have been the first one to help them. What, Yankel is crying again? Oy, I'm going *meshugga!* I stare through the glass window in the elevator door, and what do I see? My father's face! With the cap and the pockmarks, and the mole under his chin. He's cursing me already! "Yankele, you'll get it from me, wait! Don't leave any pots on the floor. And if the stand isn't closed when I come back from Hester Street, I'll toss your head over the Williamsburg Bridge. Yankel!" Who needs the elevator? I decide to walk down the stairs. "Yankel!" I grip the banister with both hands. What, did he expect me to mind the stand

for him for the rest of my life? Sure, I stood in the back
at the National and played Nuchum the Philistine, but it
was still better than staying behind my father's stand,
no? And you think I played Nuchum forever? Let Selma
call me whatever she wants! I was already acting with
Moishele Morgenstern before I met Pincus! And you
think he was the only one who praised my performances?
The *Forward* devoted half a page to me and *Muttel*.
And that's when I started buying Finkelstein's suits. After
all, what was good enough for Ben-Ami, was good enough
for me! And now I was ready to parade in front of my
father! For seven years I didn't speak a word to him, and
I always boycotted his stand. Once I wanted to show off,
and I sent one of the stage boys over to him with ten
dollars and a poster from the National, and what did he
do? He threw a pot at the stage boy and chased him for
two blocks! And the stage boy wanted compensation, so
I had to let him keep the ten dollars for himself. One
Sunday, after the matinee, I put on Finkelstein's suit and
walked over to Ludlow Street. And you should see the
way the peddlers carried on! "Muttele," they cried, "Muttele!" Honest to God, I was like a king. They left their
stands and marched behind me. But when I came to my
father's stand, I gave out a few free tickets and shooed
all the peddlers away. My father was sitting on his bench,
a pot between his knees. He was polishing the pot with
his cap. A piece of moldy bread stuck out of his pocket.
Some crumbs were caught in his beard. *"Tatele,"* I said.
You think he looked up? I started to shout. "What am I?
—a bandit? The whole East Side sees my shows, and he
won't even look at me!" I started to shake his shoulders.
The bread fell out of his pocket. It was pocked with rat-

holes, and crumbled on the ground. One of the other peddlers walked over. Who can remember his name? "Mr. Rabinowitz," he said, "please. Your father is deaf. He can't hear a word. Some *chomulehs* from Brownsville raided all the stands, and your father put up a fight. They took him behind the stand and stepped on his face. Both ears they smashed. And one eye."

I grabbed the lapels of the peddler's worn coat. "Why," I said, "why wasn't I told! What, I was in Africa? You couldn't walk over to the National and let me know?"

"Please, Mr. Rabinowitz, please. Who could afford to start up? Do I know when the *chomulehs* are coming back? Please. And would they let me in to see you? One of the biggest stars! Please."

I released his coat and he walked away. "Wait," I said, and I put five dollars in his pocket. I kneeled in front of my father and made him put down the pot. *"Tatele,"* I said, and I covered his head with the cap. Some crumbs fell from his beard and landed on my shoe. I put my head on his knees. The other peddlers began to swarm around the stand. "One of the biggest stars!" How many times did he bang my head against the wall, or chase me through the streets? I could still hear the curses and feel the blows. And you think I worried about him when I started at the National? I was glad to keep out of his sight. But only a Golem could hate his own father! So he banged my head maybe a thousand times, I'm still alive, no? Who first told me stories about Hershele Ostropolier? Not Pincus! All right, when I cried at night, he pinched me or stuck a towel over my head. But it was still better than being by myself! Once he ran off with one of his seamstresses, and my Tanta Surele wanted to have him arrested for abandoning me. But don't worry, I didn't starve! He left me enough halvah for a month! And he came back after two weeks, anyway! And you should hear the voice my father had! And he made up his own lyrics yet. How do you think he seduced all the seamstresses? With his songs! Honest to God, they wanted to make my father a cantor. But the rabbis knew that he could never reform. Who needed a scandal in *shul!* And the jokes he told! You think *Muttel* was funny? Muttel was nothing next to my father! Oy, the jokes he made up about Raisele the *rebbetzin* and Dubinsky, the traveling shoemaker! But who could repeat his stories? It would cause a scandal! And when I sat with my head on his knees, I said, "*Tatele*. I'm sorry. I'm sorry I left you with the stand." But how could he understand? Already deaf, and half-blind, who knows what those Brooklyn bandits did to him! He didn't even recognize me. I gave him back his pot. And two weeks later he died. The whole cast from the National came to his funeral. And you should see the eulogy I had the rabbi prepare! It turned out that my father was the patron of Ludlow Street! The protector of all the peddlers! What, what can't money buy for you? A wife, a bomb, a good name! For fifty dollars the rabbi sang my father's praises. And you know how many mourners I bought to say the Kaddish for him? You would never believe it. One for every *shul* on the East Side! And all the peddlers kissed my hand when they saw me. "Where could you find a son as good as Yankel!" And you think I didn't enjoy what they said? That's the way I am! Oy! I walk down the seven flights. The doorman has a message for me. From Irving? Who else! Irving, the doorman tells me, wants me to call him after I talk to Susman. But this is only half the message! On Thursday he's going over to Broad Street, and he's buying a hat for both of us. He wants me to pick out a color. The doorman looks at me. "Blue or green?" he says, "Irving told me to ask!"

"It's up to Irving," I say, and I walk out. I start to cross the street. A man carrying a violin case walks towards Irving's building. Morris?—Morris! He doesn't see me. What, he's going up to entertain for Irving? I follow him inside. I stop the doorman. He tells me that Morris lives in the building. On the second floor. I ask him for the apartment number.

"2F," he says. "Mr. Rabinowitz, should I announce you?"

"No," I say, "I'll announce myself!"

I run like a *meshuggina* up to the second floor. I stalk across the hall and find Morris' apartment. I knock on the door. He sticks his nose through the peephole, but I stand on one side. "Who is it?" he asks, "who is it?"

I disguise my voice and pretend that I'm Blumberg. You didn't know that I'm also a ventriloquist, hah? "A message," I say, "a message from Irving." He takes off the chain and opens the door. I charge inside, grab the collar of his jacket, and start to strangle him. "Help," he cries, "help!" In the dark he doesn't even recognize me, and he thinks I'm a thief. Oy, what could you steal from him?—only his life!

"Morris," I say, "it will do you no good."

And now he knows whose fingers are around his throat. His chin drops down, and he's ready to collapse. Right away I relax my grip. What, should I make him go blue in the face before I find out what the story is? There's plenty of time to break his neck! "Morris," I say, "talk! West End Avenue, hah? Talk! Who worked out for you this deal? Irving? Farbstein? Benya?"

He shrugs his narrow shoulders. "Yankele," he says, "it's only a room and a half."

I start to pull his ears. "Morris, you remember *The Phantom of the Opera?* I'll disfigure you for life!"

"Okay," he says, and he puts on the light. Honest to God, the man fell right in the middle of a *schmaltz grube!* A regular palace he has for himself. A studio couch with mahogany legs, two lamps, a desk for his fiddle, a television set with a chassis that could block out the screen at the Loew's Delancey, a Philco refrigerator that's almost as big as my whole room, and *chatchkas* on every wall. Oy, even his toilet seat shines! He stands near the door and tries to hide the television set with his fat behind. "Yankel," he says, "a glass tea?"

"Morris, don't bribe me with your tea! Talk!"

"Yankel," he says, "*they* made me do it. You think I had a choice?" And he drops his head between his shoulders like a turtle.

"Who?" I say, "what?"

He takes out his handkerchief and blows his nose. He even manages to squeeze out a tear.

"Morris," I say, "you're a fiddler, *remember,* not an actor! Now talk!"

"Yankele, the house was going down, right? And Farbstein told me to cooperate. 'Cooperate?' I said, and I was ready to throw him down the stairs. 'See my lawyer,' I told him. 'Speak to Irving!' And I thought for sure this would shut him up. He laughed in my face. And you know the way he laughs! He could creep right into

your bones. 'Irving,' he said, 'Irving is working for me!'
Who believed him? But then he showed me his lawyer
letters, signed by Irving, every one! So what could I
do? I cooperated! And I took all my instructions from
Irving. He promised me that after the marshals showed
up, he would find for me an apartment on West End
Avenue. Only cooperate! And Operation A was to get
you to move out. Farbstein wanted me to speak to you.
I should be the pacifier! But what happened? You moved
out without a fight! And after they threw Mendel out,
Irving thought you would come back and make trouble.
So he told me to hang around the Cafeteria. And what
was my mission? I should turn the whole Cafeteria
against you! 'Say anything,' Irving told me, 'make up
stories. I don't want him coming down here!' Yankel,
what could I do? Every story I told helped pay for me
my rent. Irving lets me play at all his political affairs, and
Farbstein chips in a little, so I get along. And when
Irving goes campaigning, he takes me in the car." He
opens his collar. Inside the lapels are two *Vote For Irving*
buttons. He puts out the light for a second. "See, they
glow in the dark. Your Joel coated all the buttons with a
chemical. A genius!" Now he looks down at the floor.
One eye watches me. "Yankel," he says, "you won't tell
Schmulka that I was Irving's a spy, hah? Without the
Cafeteria where do I have to go? Yankel!"

"Morris," I say, "Schmulka will never know. But
please, when you sit in Schimmel's, stay away from my
table." What, should I start strangling him again? Where's
the satisfaction? Believe me, he's worse off than I am.
To Irving he sold himself! I take out all the campaign
buttons from my pockets and drop them, one by one,

inside Morris' toilet seat. Let him flush the toilet himself!

"Morris," I say, "take a message to your boss. Tell him he can keep his allowances! Yankel can get along without him. Tell him not to worry. I won't ruin for him his campaign." What else can I say to him? That he's a skunk and a whore in his heart? He knows it himself! Morris tells me that the teapot is on the stove, but who wants to sit and drink tea with him? I walk out. Should I report back to the Cafeteria? Sure, I'll tell Schmulka all the good news! Better I'll go uptown. I'll sit in my room and watch the silverfish fight. And maybe the beetle will be able to console me? What can he do? He'll recommend poison! It's already a lost cause!

9.

The
Play's
the
Thing

Even the beetle abandoned me. I inspect all the holes around the tub, and look under the toilet seat. "Irving?" But you think he shows up? Sure, everybody deserts the sinking ship! And what about the silverfish? Honest to God, they called a truce! And now the two armies stay on opposite sides of the room. Should I be an instigator? Tell me, why should they fight for my enjoyment? Let them sit in peace! I hang Finkelstein's suit in the closet. And I stand in my underwear in front of the sink. Both of my bony knees stick out. What, this shriveled old man is Yankel the actor? They say the women fainted in the aisles when he performed. Who needed Nelson Eddy, when Yankele was on stage! Oy! Don't believe it! Selma's right. Nuchum, Nuchum the

Philistine! But if they gave me the chance, you think I couldn't play Shloimele or Yoshe Kalb? Even now! With my skinny neck and my blistered toes. I put out the light and sit on my bed. What's the use? No matter what role they gave me, people would still say, "There goes Muttel, Muttel the Thief." I sit with my elbows on my knees. I know, the minute I close my eyes I'll see my father's face, or maybe Farbstein's, and what will I dream about? One of Yupke's girls? No! I'll dream about Selma, or Irving! This is positive! Better I'll stay awake! It's cold in the room, but who has a heater? And you think the steam works? Only Irving could pick out such a room. Spite work, that's all! So what should I do? Should I act out a scene from *Muttel?* The silverfish would never allow it! They'll call off their truce and eat me alive. And I'll only drive the beetle deeper into his hole. Anyway, where's the enjoyment? I know Muttel's every move. I'll try something new. Yankel will write a play! Don't laugh! After all, what is an actor? Listen to Pincus! An actor is a puppet, a show piece. The writer and the director control the whole show. Sure, if the actor wants to complain, it's his privilege. "*Nudniks,* who stands on the stage, me or you?" And what does the director do? He shouts back! "Behave! You're only a vehicle for other people's talents. Keep your trap shut!" And if the actor gets too smart, the writer is called in, and he chops up the actor's part or throws him out of the show altogether. So you want yet I should be an actor? Who needs insults! Better I'll sit in the dark and write my play. And wait, I'll direct the whole business too! We'll need a set, no? Who can afford costumes and props? We'll use the Cafeteria! "Stage boy!" I shout. Schmulka shows up. A hammer sticks out of his pocket. He's juggling two nails with his tongue. Soon he'll complain to me that he's being overworked. Already he wipes his forehead with his sleeve. "Schmulka," I say, "*nu?* Draw the curtain. Let the play begin!" Right away he answers back. "Everybody rushes me. Did I volunteer for this job?" What, you have to pamper stage boys too? "Schmulka," I say, and I shake my fist. He runs behind the stage and draws the curtain. I can hear his hammer crash against the floor. If it was easy to find another stage boy, you think I would keep him around? *Shah!* The play is ready to begin. Oy, what kind of idiot designed the set! The counter is lopsided. The chairs and the tables look like they're ready to fall apart. And the whole floor is covered with borscht bottles and pomegranate seeds. All we need is one of Benya's bombs! "Stage designer!" I shout. Again Schmulka. Now his pants are rolled up to his knees, and he's holding a paint brush. "Schmulka," I say, "I ask for the Cafeteria, and you give me a jungle? Clean off the stage!" He climbs on the stage and starts picking up the bottles and the seeds. And when he can't carry any more bottles and all his pockets are filled up with seeds, he takes off his jacket, ties together the sleeves, and makes for himself a basket. Now he loads the basket and talks to himself. "The man is without a heart. All the work I have to do myself. You think he can't afford to hire for me an assistant? Let him burn with his bottles!" Enter Farbstein. He's wearing his black suit. One sleeve is torn. His cheeks are sucked in, and his eyes are a little glazed. "Schmulka," I scream, "get off the stage! Idiot, the show is on!" Schmulka runs off with the basket. Seeds spill out of his pockets, and a bottle drops. Farbstein advances

downstage. Is he looking for a table or a chair? His feet
scrape Schmulka's fake floorboards. Now he sits on his
knees with his shoulders slumped forward. His bald head
shines. Should I ask Schmulka to adjust the lights? His
whole body rocks back and forth, and he beats the
ground with his tiny fists, and starts to wail. Who is he
saying the Kaddish for? He looks up. Even from where
I'm standing I can see that his eyes are red. "Yankel,"
he says. What, he's talking to me yet? 'Farbstein,' I want
to tell him, 'I don't belong in the play. The show is all
yours!' "Yankel," he says again. "Yankel, please," I have
to answer him, no? He's holding up the play! *"Nu?"*
I say, "Farbstein, what can I do for you?"

"Yankel," he says, "make me a sympathetic character.
Please!"

I'm ready to laugh in his face. "Farbstein, when I'm
finished with you, the audience will chop off half your
head."

He starts to cry. On stage! "Farbstein," I say, *"shah!*
You'll ruin my production. All right, one soliloquy I'll
allow you. One!" And you should see how he thanks me!
He wants to run off the stage and kiss my hands. "Farbstein," I shout, "the play, the play!" Now he picks out a
chair and sits down. I can see. He's a little nervous. He
was never an actor before. "Yankel?" he says. He shrugs
one shoulder. His hands are trembling, and his knees
knock against the legs of the chair. "Yankel," he says,
"better I'll stand. I'm not so nervous when I stand."

"Sit, stand," I say, "but start the show!"

"The Cafeteria," he says, and now he takes a trip
across the stage. He stops in front of a table. His fingers
touch the rim. "How many times did I sit here with

Schmulka and watch Pincus play chess?" And now he pretends that he's deliberating over a move. "Pincus," he says, "push the pawn. Save the queen for later." Honest to God, the man has talent! And what do you expect? He's repeating my lines, no? He walks over to another table. "Wolf, you left your balalaika at home? What's the occasion? Your father's sick? You should have stayed home and played for him!" Now he approaches the counter. "Schimmel, no *kreplach* today? Don't get insulted, please! I love your borscht. It's such a crime to ask for *kreplach?* All right, give me the borscht." He waves his hand over the counter. "No, save the potatoes for Schmulka!" He cups both hands and pretends that he's carrying a bowl. He walks slowly. After all, he doesn't want the borscht to spill. He sits down near the counter. He looks inside the bowl. Then he pushes the borscht away. He's crying again. I know, he's only acting, but believe me, these are no crocodile tears! "What do I have from my houses?" he says. "The Cafeteria was my only home." Schmulka pokes my shoulder. He's holding a dented cymbal in each hand. "Now?" he says, "now?" I wave him away. Farbstein mumbles to himself. I stamp my feet. "Louder, louder." He stands up. "My only home."

"Schmulka," I shout.

"What? What?"

"Now!"

He drops one of the cymbals. It rolls toward the stage. "Idiot!" Enter Irving, Blumberg, Wolf, Yupke, three or four extras, and Pincus. "Schmulka, get on the stage. We need another extra!" Enter Schmulka. He joins the other extras. Pincus crosses upstage and pauses in front of a table. "Dummy," I shout, "you can't even recognize your own table? Downstage!" Pincus apologizes. "Yankel," he says, "you're the boss." Now he locates his table. "Farbstein, you're upstaging everybody. Move. Get out of the way. Stand in the corner. Go! This is not your scene."

He refuses to budge. "Not my scene? I'm the whole show. Who's on trial, me or you? Have a little respect!"

"Blumberg," I shout, "ignore him. Irving, you have your briefs?"

He winks to me. "Pop, everything's in shipshape."

"All right, everybody take a seat. Not you, Schmulka! Move your carcass behind the counter. Blumberg, to the left! Wolf, you're not in this scene. Walk off the stage! Pincus? Begin!"

Irving holds up his hand. "Pop, wait. You want people to think that I'm a turncoat? I have to explain why I'm working for the Cafeteria."

I slap my sides. Everybody, everybody wants to be a sympathetic character! "All right, Irving, explain! I'll give you two minutes. Irving, I'm counting the time."

Now he walks around Farbstein's chair. "This man," he says, "this man tried to turn me against my own father." I can see all the hate begin to register on Irving's face. His eyebrows draw together and almost meet. His lips are already parched, and one of his cheeks collapse. 'Irving,' I want to say, 'all this for me?' The sunken cheek begins to quiver, and Irving holds his hand over his face. "Farbstein," he says, "you're a fiend. Schmulka, throw him in the cellar. Let him live with the rats. He's not fit for human company."

Farbstein picks up his chair. "Yankel, no more, you

hear? I'm walking out of the play. Let him choke on his lines!" He turns his head sharply towards Pincus. "I turned him against his father, hah? He should live so! The whole business was his idea! Honest to God, I'm innocent!"

"Farbstein," I say, "shut up! Take the chair back to your place."

"And what if I refuse? Without me who will you use for a villain? I'm the central character, no? Tell him to apologize. Yankel, you need me in the play!"

Irving is ready to cooperate. After all, he doesn't want the play to fall apart. But I tell him, "No!" What, you think Farbstein is angry? He's enjoying his performance.

Now Pincus complains. "Yankel, can we stand on stage without a play?"

"Midget," I say, "we don't need you for a mediator. I'll settle the dispute by myself." Schmulka is whispering to one of the extras. I stand up and shout. Yankel the Thunderer! "All of you, shut up! I'll replace the whole cast. I mean it!" The extras stand at attention. Blumberg takes out Irving's briefs and tries to look busy. His hands are shaking. Pincus sits without making a sound. Farbstein tiptoes across the stage and moves his chair back into position. Irving looks at the ceiling. Only Yupke is relaxed. He's sleeping under his table. And why should I disturb him? Don't worry, when it comes time for him to perform, he'll get from me a cue! "Now," I say, "no more monkey business. I want the play to proceed without intrusions. Pincus, convene the court."

Pincus removes the salt shaker from his table. Then he spreads apart his elbows, rubs the boil on his nose, and says, "Bring over the defendant."

"Pincus," I shout, "you're fouling up my staging. Let the spider stay where he is." Farbstein claps his hands over his knees. *"Nu?"* he says, "what's the charge?"

Irving signals to me. "Pop, it's in the bag. We'll hit him with everything. Manslaughter, larceny, kidnaping, pimping, attempting to overthrow the Cafeteria. Pop, the works. Leave it to me!"

"I protest," Farbstein says, "I protest! Overthrow the Cafeteria? Who! Why? Because I wanted to buy up the mortgage? Since when is this illegal? Irving, you yourself signed for me all the papers."

"Immaterial," Irving shouts. "I was working then in another capacity. I'm completely exonerated. Coercion! Farbstein, you forced me to act in your behalf."

"Forced him he says. Forced him! Irving, who taught you to tell such lies?" Should I answer for Irving? "You planned the whole deal! Somebody, somebody speak for me. Tillie! Tillie!"

"Farbstein," Pincus says, "pipe down. This isn't the National Theatre!"

Believe me, it's a pleasure to write such a play! 'Irving,' I want to say, 'give it to him!' But I have to pretend that I'm fair, no? An author can't take sides. He has to stick with all his characters. Farbstein, wait. This scene is only an appetizer. When I'm finished with you. . . . Pincus is reprimanding me already.

"Yankel," he says, "keep your nose out of our affairs. Irving, your witnesses!"

Now Schmulka stands behind the counter and shouts, "The Cafeteria calls Tillie!"

Farbstein almost falls out of his chair. "My Tillie,"

he says, "a witness for the Cafeteria? What is she charging me with?"

Irving closes in. He's ready for the kill. "Kidnaping," he says, "statutory rape, and living off the earnings of prostitution." His words fall on Farbstein like hammer blows. "My Tillie?" He draws his shoulders together and looks around for some place to hide. Yupke crawls out from under his table. He whirls his head in Farbstein's direction. Honest to God, the way the lights are working, the head is on fire! "A pimp, a pimp," Yupke says. "I'm ready to testify. Tillie rented out a room at the *Draidl*. Farbstein financed her. A pimp!" He crawls back under the table. Farbstein starts whacking his bald head with his tiny fists. "Lies, lies!" His temples gleam.

Schmulka shouts out again, "The Cafeteria calls Tillie!"

"Nu?" Pincus says, "where's the witness!"

"Pop," Irving says, "what's the catch? That's your job! Create the characters! Pop, put Tillie on stage. You're making a fool out of me. Pop, we'll lose the case." Irving has his handkerchief out. He's in trouble, I know. But what can I do? Create characters he says. What, does he think it's like taking an enema? Poof! "Irving, I'll try for you." I squeeze, but nothing comes out! "Tillie, Tillie. Where is she?"

"Pop, if not Tillie, then at least give me Mendel or Fishbein. How can we get a conviction without witnesses!"

Oy, I can see already that the play is getting out of hand. You think I have any control? "Fishie? Mendele?" Nobody shows up! Irving wants witnesses, what can I do?

"Pop, Pop!"

Now Schmulka gets into the act. He tries to hide his smile with his fist. "The Cafeteria," he says, "the Cafeteria calls Yankel!"

"*Me?* Schmulka, you're making a mistake. I'm not in this play. How can I be a witness?" The three extras walk off the stage. I start to shout like a *meshuggina*. I threaten the whole cast. You think they're frightened? My legs are shaking. The three extras start to drag me towards the stage. "Wait," I say, "wait. If I'm going on stage, let me at least put on Finkelstein's suit. Irving, I have to warm up. Give me a chance to rehearse."

"Pop, who has time?"

"Irving," I say, "will occur a calamity on stage. Without a director. Without an author. What kind of play?" The bandits station me in front of Pincus' table. Farbstein is shouting at me. "That's him! That's him!"

"Who? What?" I plead with Pincus. "Midget, please." The boil on his nose begins to swell. He turns his head away.

"Shut him up," Farbstein says, "shut him up."

I didn't say a word. Irving reads off the charges.

"Abandonment, desertion . . ." Enter Clara, Tillie, Mendel, Fishie, my father . . . All with bitter, rankled faces. "I deny everything. It's my play! Everybody, walk off the stage. Walk . . ." Mendele is polishing his samovar. Clara is holding her bridal veil. Tillie is stuffing straw inside the sagging cups of her brassière. Fishie is scratching his swollen ankles. My father is picking crumbs from his beard. Irving joins them. He's wearing a putty nose and a sailor suit. Hershele. "Pincus," I shout, "disband the court." Farbstein hisses. I whirl around and face the witnesses. "I didn't do a thing!" I walk over to my father and clasp his knees. His eyes are hollowed out. Ants swarm inside the empty sockets and attack his chin and the folds of his ears. Mendele sings to himself. Someone presses my shoulders to the ground. My elbows bang against the floorboards. Farbstein stands over me. His jaw seems gigantic. The tables and chairs start to move. The counter slides forward. Downstage! Upstage! I hear myself shouting. The stage starts to crumble. I'm riding through a tunnel. *Mommenu,* I'm inside Yudel's droshky! I can see the gleaming flanks of the horses. The pendants attached to their bridles flap crazily in the wind. "Coachman," Yudel shouts, "faster, faster." He's wearing hobnailed boots and a black caftan. He puts one arm around me. My head leans against his shoulder. Our knees touch. He unbuttons my shirt. His rings shine in the dark. The coachman sticks his head through one of the windows. Farbstein. Farbstein. I scream. I'm sitting on the floor. I can hear the pipes belch under the sink. The doorknob starts to rattle. Who knows? Maybe there's a demon inside. I shout at the doorknob. "Rattle all you want." It answers me back. "Yankel, how long will I have to wait?" I stand up, shaky knees or not! "Lena?"

"Who were you expecting? Molly Picon maybe?"

I open the door for her.

"Lena," I say, "let me put on my suit."

She slaps her forehead. "He's embarrassed yet! Yankel, I don't see you for one day and already we're strangers?" She looks around the room. "Such a mess! Susman was here?" Right away she sits down on my bed.

Leave it to Lena! What, who has the strength to take off her girdle? Yankel is pooped! What can I do? She starts undressing herself!

"Lena," I say, "what, it's after midnight?"

"Midnight?" she says. "Yankel, you want the clock to sit and wait for you? The morning is already over!"

Oy! I spent the whole night working on my play? Who could believe it! We never even finished the first act! "Lena," I say, "I have important business at the Center."

"Yankel," she says, "the business can wait! Here, unhook me!"

So I play Muttel for Lena, and after we act out two scenes on my bed, she straps on her girdle, and makes me a glass of tea.

"Lena," I say, "you were at the Center before? The Torch was there?"

"The Torch?"

"Benya, Benya! Susman's broker. Schwartz!"

And I explain to Lena my plan. "Kapel put the embargo on me. So who can go inside? And if Susman knows I'm around, it will be the end of me. Lena, bring the Torch outside. Tell him Yankel wants to speak to him. And Lena, if he refuses, tell him I'll make an appeal to Susman herself!"

We walk over to the Center. Lena gives me a kiss for good luck. "Yankel," she says, "don't worry, I'll bring the broker out." What can you do? Lena loves espionage! I stand behind a tree and wait for the Torch. How can he refuse me? He's inheriting Susman's seven houses! He walks outside. He's wearing a silk suit, with a handkerchief in his pocket. The handkerchief matches his tie and socks, and his belt buckle shines. Who do you think bought him the outfit? Susman, of course! Benya never knew from handkerchiefs! I call him over. "Benya!"

You think he's happy to see me? I should worry! I can tell right away. Benya is without his bombs! And with such a suit would he carry around a knife? "Benya," I say again. Oy, I hope the whole Center hears me!

"Yankel," he says. "The Torch is retired. Permanent!"

"Sure," I say, "with Susman for a backer, why not?"

His eyebrows hang down. "You paged me for a purpose, no?"

"Look at him!" I say. "With me he plays Ishkele the Innocent! Benya, Fishie's right-hand man, and you run out? You should see him in his cage. Then you would know! And he was worrying yet about his Benya. 'Yankel, tell him I'm all right!' "

Benya takes out his handkerchief. Now he's using Irving's tactics! "Yankel," he says, "all my life I am waiting for such an opportunity, and you think now I'm not going to take it? How many Susmans can you find at one Center?"

"Benya, please, who wants to interfere with your romance! Susman is yours! But get from her the money for Fishie's bail!"

"No," he says, "no. I can't afford to get involved. If Susman finds out that I am mixed up with Fishie, she will cancel all the arrangements. A broker all right, but not a gangster!"

"Benya!" He turns on me his back. "You want him to rot in Raymond Street?"

"Yankel, I can't do a thing. I'm going with Susman

tomorrow to Miami Beach." He looks at me for a second. "Yankel, when I come back from Miami, then I'll bail him out!"

"Benya, who knows when you'll come back. With Susman a honeymoon could last for a year! Benya, try! Tell her it's for a friend who wants to start a business. You'll get back every cent. You want collateral? Count on the Cafeteria! I'll get Schimmel to sign! Benya?"

"Yankel," he says, "goodbye!" One of his shoulders is shaking. He tries to fold the handkerchief. It drops on the ground. I pick it up for him, fold over the corners, and put it in his pocket. "Yankel," he says, "I promise. When I come back." He walks back to the center. I signal to Lena. She comes out.

"Yankel," she says, "the plan worked?"

"By me when does a plan ever work? Lena, you have a dollar to lend me? I need it for a cab."

"Yankele, where are you flying?"

"To the Elsmere!" Sure, I'll join Prince Manishevitz's troupe. What else can I do? Maybe he'll give me an advance! Oy, such a low-life! But at least I'll be able to make some money for Fishie's bail. Lena takes out two dollars from her purse. "Yankele," she says, "here. Maybe you'll need a little extra. The way cab drivers are today, they always double the fare. When will you be back? Today? Tomorrow?"

We kiss in the middle of the street. "Lena, who knows when I'll be back? With Yankel everything is possible! When I settle my business, Lena, don't worry, I'll look for you!"

She buttons my coat. "Yankel, take care." She finds for me a cab. You think we stop kissing? The cab driver gives us both dirty looks. "Mr.," Lena tells him, "the meter's running, no? So turn around and count off the nickels!" Finally she pushes me into the cab. "Driver," I shout, "take me to the Bronx." Lena waves to me. "Yankele, keep your coat buttoned. Take care."

The driver drops me off in front of the Elsmere. I run over to the ticket booth. Already people are lined up for the Sunday matinee. I knock on the window of the booth. *"Nudnik,"* I say, "tell your boss that Yankel Rabinowitz of the National is looking for him." The ticket seller holds up his hands. "How can I leave the booth?"

"Go," I say, "tell the Prince I'm waiting."

The ticket seller locks up the booth and runs inside the theatre. He comes back in a minute. He walks past me without a word and hides himself inside the booth.

"Nu?" I say.

And you should see the look he gives me! "Prince Manischevitz doesn't know any Yankel Rabinowitz!"

"What?" I say, "what?" An amateur, and he snubs me yet! Wait! I walk backstage and find the Prince's dressing room. He's inside with Olga, his wife.

"Manischevitz," I say, "first you steal my routine, and then you refuse to recognize me! No wonder they threw you out from the Union!"

Oy, even with all his make-up, you can see every wrinkle on his face. His dentures sit in a cup on his dressing table. And with his teeth inside the cup, his mouth looks just like a scab. All right, my face has its own history, but with a little powder on each cheek, I could still play Muttel any day! And believe me, I'm older yet than the Prince! "Rabinowitz," he says, "what can I do for you?"

"Manischevitz, you're a lucky man. I've decided to come out of retirement. I was here Friday night. Why shouldn't I say it? Your show is a flop! Boris, you need me in your troupe!"

He leans back and laughs. His sucked in cheeks start to whistle. "Olga," he says, "you hear him? We need him in the troupe! The star of Second Avenue! Pincus runs him off the stage, and now he wants to make his comeback in the Bronx!" He slaps the dressing table and the dentures rattle in the jar. Olga puts her arm around his shoulder.

"Manischevitz," I say, "reconsider. My feud with Pincus has nothing to do with my career!" Sure, it's a lie, but I have to take insults from this *schmendrik!* "You think I couldn't get a show at the Anderson or the Alliance? Boris, with me in your troupe, they'll call you back to Second Avenue. This is positive!"

"Second Avenue?" he says. "Ghost towns we don't need! I'm taking the troupe to Montreal." He starts powdering his face. "Rabinowitz, the interview is over!" Olga opens the door.

I would like to strangle them both, but what can I do? And I wanted to join his troupe yet! Oy, how could I stand on the same stage with Prince Manischevitz! I walk out of the theatre. One name beats like a pulse inside my head. *Pincus.* A double row forms outside the theatre. They're waiting for the *Prince.* Pincus. Sure, Joan of Arc had her voices, and I have my pulse beats. Pincus! What can I do? He's the only one! Let Farbstein, and Irving, and the Raymond Street jail band together. The midget could rout them in a minute. What does Muttel say in the second act? Sometimes it pays better to ally yourself with an enemy, than with a friend! And what's good enough for Muttel, is also good enough for me! All right, the man ruined my career, but now is the time to be proud? Can he help out Fishie? This is what counts! We'll call a temporary truce. What, who gave him permission to lock himself in his room, when Fishie sits in jail? Wait!

10.

Pincus

Once, after I came back from a week-end trip, I found all the drawers open, and half the furniture was missing. Bandits? No! Clara took Irving and the furniture and moved out! Where did she go? It took Yupke's agents a week to locate her. She rented out a room on Attorney Street. You think I wanted her back? But the whole Second Avenue was laughing at me. Cuckold they called me. Everybody thought for sure that she had Pishkele the plumber for a protector. So I ran over to Attorney Street. Three locks she had on the door! And when I began to shout, she told me that she was sending Irving down the fire escape for the police. So I called her a whore and went home. Let Pishkele provide for her! And now I shuttled back and forth from the Cafeteria to the *Draidl*. And Yupke wouldn't leave me alone. I had to

break in for him all his new girls. That was my special
job! Yankel the stud! What could I do? Pincus wasn't
around! He was too busy chasing after his chorus girl.
Mommenu, you should see the way the man declined!
He would appear now once a week at the Cafeteria, and
half the time he was in a trance. "Shaindele, Shaindele."
Schimmel already had the shits! He didn't dare to take
a step away from the toilet seat. And right away Schmulka
formed a committee. "Yankel, do something! He walks
back and forth like a spook. He's ruining for us our
trade! Schimmel or not, I'll throw him out from the Cafeteria." But what could I do? The midget was in love!
Three times a day he wrote poems to her. *Shaindele*. And
you think she read them? Oy, was this a Shaindele! She
used the poems for doilies! How do I know? What, how
many times did I sit with her and the other chorus girls
and drink tea! I'm telling you, the midget was insane.
The biggest actresses fell in love with him, one after the
other. Like flies! But he wanted only Shaindele! And
when he wrote her messages, who do you think he picked
out to deliver them? Me! And when I appeared at the
dressing room with Pincus' messages, she chased out all
the other chorus girls, closed the curtain and dragged me
over to the couch. Why should I lie? You think I didn't
enjoy myself! A John Alden I never was, and I'll never
be! And I tried to warn him. "Pincus, she's not for you."
Would he listen to me? He chased me out of his room.
And why do you think I went with Shaindele to the Catskills? Call it spitework, who's stopping you! Honest to
God, I wanted him to find out! I wanted to show him once
and for all what he could expect from his Shaindele.
But don't think Yankel sacrificed himself! The girl wore

me out! What, at least at the *Silver Draidl* I had time to relax. Shaindele wouldn't let me crawl out of bed for a second. Oy, she pinched me black and blue! What for did she need to be a chorus girl? She could have made a fortune for Yupke and herself! And when I came back, you think I didn't expect Pincus to give me hell? I told half of Second Avenue that Shaindele was taking me to the Catskills. I figured the midget would curse me out in front of the Cafeteria, and threaten to convene the court, and then buy me a knish and say, "Yankele, I learned my lesson!" But like a dunce I figured wrong! He didn't even bother with the court. He spit in my face and walked out of the Cafeteria. And you think Schimmel and Schmulka were on my side? Schmulka refused to serve me for a week. But even he didn't expect the midget to keep it up. And when Pincus gave me the business in the *Forward* and the *Day,* Schmulka went over to Norfolk Street and tried to talk to him. The midget wouldn't even let him in. "Yankel," he said, "what can I do?" And after all the producers put the embargo on me, Schimmel called me over. "Yankel, enough is enough! Maybe he's waiting for you to make up with him? You know the way he is!" So the next day, when Pincus came into the Cafeteria, Schimmel made me walk over to his table. "Shake," Schimmel said, "what, two children?" You think I wasn't ready to apologize? I even prepared a little speech. But he wouldn't even look at me! He peeled his potato and dropped it into the borscht. "Pincus," I said. And how did he answer me? He belched in my face! What, you think I'm made from stone? I walked out of the Cafeteria. And a week later I put on a beard and played Maurie the Meshuggina at the Clinton. All right, maybe next to Ben-Ami, *Muttel the Thief* was vaudeville. Who says no! But how could you compare Muttele with Maurie the Meshuggina! Maurie was *dreck* altogether! All the other actors—actors? Call them better clowns—slapped my buttocks with little bats, and I had to run across the stage and pull my beard. What, this was my reward for twenty years' work at the National? And believe me, it wasn't my sore behind that made me cancel my contract! Better I should retire than spend my time at the Clinton Street! And you think I didn't look for work? Oy, you could never imagine in your life how many schemes I tried! First Schmulka found for me an agent. That's what I needed with all my *tzuris!* An agent yet I had to support! Honest to God, I was his only client! Koningsberg! And who was Koningsberg? Believe me, it's not so easy to answer! Maybe forty years ago he was a rabbinical student in Odessa for a month or two, but everyone still called him "Rabbi." And the man had more careers than Pincus had suits! A smuggler, a marriage broker, a pimp, a horse thief, a professional bridegroom, who can name them all! "The Rabbi," Schmulka told me, "is a man of many talents." And now, in his old age, he decided to be an agent! And what was the Rabbi's advice? "Yankel," he told me, "Hollyvoot!" Oy! Right away he made me change my name. Poof! Jack Rabin, formerly of the Jewish stage. But who had money to run to Hollywood? And I would have to pay yet his fare. So he forgot about Hollywood and got in touch with WEVD. All right, let the National lock me out, I could still act on the radio, no? But you think the Rabbi found for me a dramatic part? Commercials they wanted me to do. For Goldberg's Haberdashery Stores. And I had to make up

my own jingles yet! After Jennie Goldstein sang about
her Yiddishe Mamma, I ran over to the microphone and
shouted like a *meshuggina,* "Men, boys, Goldberg's,
Goldberg's is the store for you! A suit, a hat, a coat . . ."
Oy, who wants to remember the lines! And every time
I walked into the Cafeteria, Schmulka touched his knees
and said, *"Shah,* the Haberdashery Man is here!" I was
a regular celebrity! The whole Cafeteria wanted dis-
count cards for Goldberg's Clinton Street store. And
I had to wear yet his suits! That was part of the deal!
Sure, I had heartaches and gall bladder attacks, and the
Rabbi lived and laughed. Goldberg furnished him from
head to toe, and Farbstein found for him an apartment
on East Broadway. "Yankel," he told me, "I'm ready
to branch out." And every Tuesday he held auditions in
the Cafeteria, and after three or four weeks, he rounded
up maybe twenty new clients. A harmonica player with
one leg, a female accordionist with a pushed-in face,
don't ask! Honest to God, Prince Manischevitz was one
of his clients! And you think he found jobs for them?
But they still had to pay him his fee! A swindler, what
can you do? But how long could I stand like a monkey
in front of the microphone? So I gave Goldberg back
all his suits, and packed him in together with the Rabbi!
Let Koningsberg collect from his other clients! And now
I became a boarder at the Cafeteria. What, you think
I could have survived without Schimmel's sour cream
and borscht? And Schmulka gave me pocket money too.
Schimmel wanted to bring me over to Pincus' table again,
but this time I rebelled. "No," I said, and I made sure
that the midget heard me. He was playing chess with
Morris. "Let the man have his satisfaction. What else

would he have to do if he didn't spend his time crucifying me!" Pincus dropped one of his chess pieces, but he didn't look up once from the table. Morris told me later that Pincus played a terrible game. He traded both rooks for a bishop, and gave away his queen for free! Schmulka swore that the game was fixed! "When did you ever see Pincus play like that?" And the next day Pincus amazed the whole Cafeteria. It was Tuesday, and the midget was wearing his Wednesday suit! I should worry! I extra stayed away from the Cafeteria. I wanted to avoid him. And Schmulka had to deliver Schimmel's borscht to my door. But Gershen the Gonef began to spread stories about Pishke and Clara, and after Morris told me the news, I fortified myself with some vodka, and ran over to Attorney Street. I waited in the hall like a spider, and when Clara showed up with her shopping bag, I followed her up the stairs. And after she opened up the door, I dragged her inside. "Pishke, heh?" I said, and I banged her head against the wall. "Pishke!" But the plumber wasn't there. And it's a lucky thing for me. With his pipes and his wrenches, he could have fixed me for good. But she didn't need Pishke for a protector? Irving was around! What, you think he was still Hershele with the putty nose? He was already sixteen years old! Believe me, he didn't hide under the table! He started knocking my shoulders with a seltzer bottle. "Pop," he said, "lay off!" All right, if I couldn't act on stage, off stage would have to do! You should see the performance! First I slapped my head. "A son should hit his father? This I never heard!" Right away he put down the seltzer bottle. And I gave Clara an extra bang! Then I clapped my hands, picked out a chair, and sat with my head over my lap. *"Gottenu!"*

Sure, I gave them the whole routine! Irving had to find for me a handkerchief. But you think Clara was a dope? She knew right away I was faking! She let me finish the performance, and then she picked up a broom. What could I do? If I took the broom away from her and broke it over her head, Irving would find out in a minute that my whole performance was a put-up job. And his seltzer bottle was still sitting on the floor. So I let Clara bombard me with the broom, and I kept up my act. "Ma," Irving said, "you'll split open his head!" 'Irving,' I wanted to say, 'don't give her any ideas!' Finally, after she hit me fifty or sixty times, Irving took the broom away from her. Clara ran into the bedroom. "Irving," she said, "make up your mind. Send him away or I'm moving out." Irving slapped his sides. "Me they made a referee! Ma, talk to him. Maybe . . ." Clara closed her door. "Pop," Irving said, "you better go." So I wiped my eyes and walked out. "Pop, I'll try and talk to her. Pop?" I had to show him I was offended, no? So I didn't even answer him back. Oy, my legs and shoulders were so sore from Clara's sixty knocks, it took me an hour to get home. And the next day Irving showed up. He had with him a package. Chicken soup with *kreplach*. "Irving," I said, "Clara knows you brought me the soup?" He wouldn't answer me. I was hungry like a dog, but Yankel the dope wanted satisfaction. So I spilled the soup into the sink. The *kreplach* clogged the drain. I could hear my stomach groan. Irving wanted to give me fifty cents. "Pop," he said, "I can afford it." Sure, every day, after school, he delivered orders for that low-life, Gluck the druggist. You could be sure of one thing when you ordered medicine from Gluck. Cured or not, you always ended up with diarrhea! Who knows how many times the man lost his license, but Farbstein always bailed him out. The spider owned half interest in Gluck's store! And you think it didn't hurt me to take from Irving the fifty cents? "Irving," I said, "wait, I'll make you out an IOU."

"Pop," he said, "Pop." And every Tuesday I found fifty cents under my door in an envelope marked "Gluck." And now you know the truth. For the past twenty-five years Irving has kept me alive! What could I do? The midget kept up with his hatchet job! Sure, I saved all his articles. But you think I need my scrapbook? I remember every word! "Boris Bookbinder's infantile performance in *The Organ Grinder* reminded me of the *late* Yankel Rabinowitz. Thank God his ghost no longer haunts the National. I fell asleep after the first act." Sure, that's the way Pincus panned a show. He would start to snore in the middle of the performance. You want to hear more? Wait! "What ever happened to Yankele? Has he joined the fish peddlers' association? Or is he the new singing waiter at Moskowitz and Lupowitz?" "Perlmutter is casting again for the *Forward Follies*. Was it our Yankele I saw delivering bagels to one of Perlmutter's chorus girls?" Oy, what that man did to me! I was ashamed to walk out in the street! "Apologize," Schmulka warned me, "before he eats you up alive." No! Better I'll spit blood before I apologize to him! So I sat day and night in my room. And then Koningsberg started pestering me. He would appear at my door every other day. "Yankele? Perlmutter is taking his troupe to Montevideo. They're going to tour the whole Argentine. Yankel, I fixed it with him. We'll smuggle you on the boat. The midget will never know. And what can he do to you in

Montevideo? Who knows, maybe you'll start your own troupe. Yankel, Perlmutter will pay for you the passage!" You think I wasn't tempted to go? But why should I run away like a thief! So I stayed on Second Avenue. And Perlmutter collected a million in Montevideo and Buenos Aires. And what did I collect sitting in my room? Heartaches and boils on my behind!

Goldfarb's grocery is gone, but Bendelberg's monuments still occupies half of Norfolk Street. Bendelberg's Memorials, Inc. Free Parking For Our Customers. 'Bendelberg,' I want to say, 'believe me, your customers have already parked themselves!' On The Same Block Since 1899. I look at the stones inside the window. In Our Hearts You Live Forever. A map of Israel is pasted on the window. A doll's head sits on the steps of the abandoned Lithuanian synagogue. Bendelberg is branching out! Next year he's going to convert the synagogue into another showroom. After all, he needs the space. Where can he put all the stones! Pincus' house stands near the synagogue. Half the windows are already boarded, and the walls have started to peel. A girl is sitting on the fire escape. Her skirt is pulled up over her knees, and I can already see the hem of her underpants. What, in my old age I should become yet a Peeping Tom! I walk inside. The whole hallway is cluttered with garbage cans. A regular arsenal! Right away I name the cans, "Schimmel, Schmulka, Maurie, Muttel, and Shloime," and I walk up to the second floor. Honest to God, the cockroaches are using the banisters for a highway! I stand outside Pincus' door. I can feel my heart pound. Oy, I think I'm catching Schimmel's shits! Yankel, I tell myself, what, you're going to let the midget make you nervous? Go, knock on his door! What can I do? My knuckles refuse to knock! *Meshuggina,* figure out first a strategy! You think it's so easy to maneuver the midget? Yankele, hide your feelings. Throw away your heart, or put it at least between your kidneys. You want from him a favor, no? Be nice! Let him think you came over to make up with him. Smile. Kiss his hand. You should worry! Now I knock on the door. "Midget, open up!" I hear a noise inside the room. Sure, the beetles and the bedbugs are running for cover. You think I bother to knock again? For Pincus one knock is enough! "Pincus, you hear?" I go to work on the doorknob, but it drops out of its socket and bangs my toes. The war didn't even begin, and I'm already a casualty! What, you expect me to stand outside his door forever? "Pincus, I'm lighting a match. Honest to God, I'll burn you out together with the bedbugs!" Go threaten the midget! You think it will get you anywhere? While the house burns down, he'll sit inside his bathtub reading *The Captain's Daughter,* or muse over Pushkin's duel for the thousandth time. What could he be doing now? Is he polishing his chess pieces? No, the midget hasn't played chess in twenty years! Maybe he's teaching the bedbugs how to sing? "Pincus?" Oy, let him stand on his head and pick the dirt out of his bellybutton! You think it bothers me? I stand with my nose next to the door. "Midget, goodbye! Sit, sit in your room, Yankel is going!" I walk towards the banister. I hear him scurry across the room like a rat. At least now I know he's alive! "Goodbye!" The door opens. I walk inside. He's wearing a nightshirt that hangs below his knees. His tiny feet are spread out like a duck, and his eyes are half-closed. What can I say to him? Honest to God, I want to run home! And you think my room is in bad shape, hah? His books are piled all over the floor. And in the corner, on top of one pile, sits an empty Pepsi-Cola bottle, like a long-necked Humpty Dumpty who knows he's ready to fall. But it's not the books and the Pepsi-Cola bottle that bothers me! All right, thirty years ago, when I sat in his room, he at least put a cover on his bed, and kept a picture of Lermontov on the wall, and never let the cock-roaches get the upper hand. Now the cockroaches control the woodwork and the walls, and his bed looks like a regular three-ring circus. In the middle sits Pincus' pil-low, with a Flit gun and a slice of pumpernickel for com-panions. Near the headboard you can find a notebook with a cover that's ready to peel, a rotten apple with an old man's face, and a dented pen without a point or a cap. Even Mendele in his better days would never have handled such a pen! But if you're looking for the main attraction, you have to walk over to the footboard. There, waiting to dry, is Pincus' union suit, with the patched knees and the stretched ankle bands. Honest to God, it's like meeting an old friend! The midget never went anywhere without his union suit! And when he entertained Morris or me in his room, you think he bothered wearing one of Finkelstein's suits? Oy! I'm ready to wink at the patched knees. I walk around the piles of books—who wants to disturb the Pepsi-Cola bottle?—and sit down on the bed. I can feel the springs sag under my behind. He sits on the other side of the bed. Two warriors at a council! What, he expects me to say the first word? The boil on his nose begins to shine. He pretends that he's looking at the floor. But I can tell.

The man is watching my every move! God forbid, if I should sneeze or cough, he would fall right off the bed. 'Pincus,' I want to say, 'what, you lost your tongue?' What can I do? He refuses to open his mouth! So I slap the headboard and say, "Pincus, you shouldn't think I came here to call a truce. It's too late now for reconciliations. But you know what happened to Fishie. So make one appearance at the Cafeteria and then goodbye and good luck." You think my words have any effect? He looks at me like I'm a loon. "What," I say, "Schmulka didn't explain you the situation? Schimmel is the only one who can pay Fishie's bail. But he won't come out of his room until you show your face. Midget, I have to write out the words for you on the wall?" Honest to God, I'm ready to tear out my hair. "Hate me all you want, you think it bothers me? Just show your face!" Now he pulls up the hem of his nightshirt, and knocks his knees together. I can see all the veins on his calves. "Pincus, you know I have a temper. Cooperate!" I grab both ankle bands of his union suit. "Here, put on your *gatkehs,* and come!" What can you do with the man? Like Gandhi he sits! Does he want me to crawl along the floor and beg him? Oy, the cockroaches would eat me alive! "Midget," I say, and I salaam to him, with both thumbs touching my nose. "Are you satisfied?" All right, whatever he wants to hear, I'll say! You think it bothers me? "Pincus, Yankel apologizes." What, he's deaf to the bargain! I say it again! "Pincus . . ." One giant tear leaks out of his left eye, glides over the bumps and pits near his nostril, and lands on his chin. He pinches his fingers together and catches the tear, just like a star. At least I know now he's not a zombie! He still refuses to talk!

I thrust my face halfway across the bed. "Here," I say, "spit on me again. *Nu?* Get for yourself some satisfaction. Believe me, this is your last chance." And now, for the first time, he smiles. And when the midget smiles, it's already a victory! You think his lips move? The folds under his eyes come together, and each eyelash salutes the other. What can you do? This is what he calls a smile! But who can get him to open his mouth? I lean against the headboard.

"Yankele."

Oy, it's a miracle!

"You were always a *meshuggina!*"

Yankel changed his mind! I have to hear insults yet? Let him remain a zombie better and keep his trap shut! "Meshuggina, hah? Pincus, you should know! If I don't talk to you for another twenty-five years, it wouldn't bother me for a minute! Please, if you see me in the street, walk in the other direction."

"Nu?" he says, and now he talks to his knees. "Who needed Karamazov, the dancing bear, when I had Yankele all the time!"

"Sure, I was for you a puppet. When you said sing, Yankele sang. Pincus' personal buffoon! You think I had to play Maurie at the Clinton Street? You slapped my behind for twenty years! Yankele, the clown from Schimmel's Cafeteria. Pincus, give the word. The Cafeteria is waiting. What, a song from *Muttel?* Or should I climb better on the counter with a glass of borscht on my head and do the *kazatska* for you? No! Schmulka, bring out the chess board. Let the midget amuse himself! Give him a chance to steal my pawns one by one, and move his pieces across the board like a pack of wolves." He wipes his eyes with the sleeve of his nightshirt. "Every king needs his fool. Pincus, you think I really minded your reviews? You were right! Yankel *was* a toad without talent! He *should* have been a member of the fish peddlers' association. That's where he belonged! So why did you wait twenty years? You couldn't tell me from the beginning? What, you wanted revenge? I should have let you chase after Shaindele for the rest of your life! Then you would have known what it means to be a buffoon. Shaindele's *schmendrik!* I should have told her to put a leash around your neck and let the other girls pinch your cheeks and pat your behind. And she would have said to me, 'Yankel, take him out for a walk. I don't want him to pee in the dressing room. The girls will have a fit!' And I would have dragged you over to one of the lots on Chrystie Street, and said, 'Pincus, piss! Piss to your heart's content!' "

And now he closes one eye, and honest to God, the other eye looks like it's ready to move over to the middle of his head. A Cyclops, what can you do? "Yankele," he says, "even without Shaindele, I was always the buffoon! Not you! You think I loved her? I was playing a part! Yankel, I always envied you."

Should I laugh in his face? I slap my sides and the bed almost collapses. "Me he envied! Maurie the Meshuggina, and Nuchum, Nuchum the Philistine!"

"I would have given up twenty years and all my reviews to play Maurie at the Clinton for a week. Maurie! I would have worn ten beards gladly and stuck out my behind, and offered everyone in the theatre a free shot. Paddle me, with pleasure! Yankel, I would have bought myself a brassière and danced next to Shaindele in the

Forward Follies! Anything! And when Duvie Pinchuk put on *Muttel* at the National, I didn't sleep for a week. Even Schimmel's borscht couldn't tempt me. The whole Cafeteria thought that I was worrying about my Yankele. 'Pincus,' Schmulka told me, 'the man is a natural for the part. You think he has to play Muttele? He is Muttel! And with the new material that you added to the show, how can he go wrong?' Yankel, the whole time I was thinking only about one thing. I wanted to play *Berkowitz*, your bodyguard!"

"Berkowitz? Pincus, you used to . . ."

"I know. Now you see me for what I am. 'Better a fish peddler than an actor! What is he? The director's stooge!' I drove half of Perlmutter's troupe off the stage, and all the time I was jealous! Midget you called me? Monster is a better word!"

"Pincus, such a *tzimis* you had to make? Believe me, you didn't miss a thing! But if you wanted so much to be an actor, why didn't you ask Duvie to sign you up?"

"Sure," he says, "sure," and he thumps his kneecaps with his tiny fists. "You think I wanted the whole world to learn about my lunacy? I kept it better to myself." He leans over and touches the hump on his back. "They would have thrown me into the pit and eaten me alive. Hirschhorn and all the other critics would have taken their revenge. And Schimmel would have banished me for life. 'One actor is enough!' So I played my parts off the stage." He stands up and walks across the room. The floorboards squeak under his bare feet. He complains about his bunions and corns, and then he marches back to the bed. *"Shaindele,"* he says, "I was acting all the time. If I ran after Sarah Nemerov or Bella Winkler, who would have noticed me? 'So what?' they would have said, 'Pincus is having an affair.' So I picked out Shaindele. And right away everybody turned around. The critic and the showgirl!"

"Pincus, no stories! He follows her around like a dog, and he expects me to believe that it was a put-up job! Even Ben-Ami could never act out such a part. Your eyes were ready to pop out. And who delivered your messages three times a day?"

"Yankel, you know yourself. Sometimes an actor gets carried away. That's always the danger. I fell in love with my own part. I wanted everyone to see how Shaindele was making me suffer. So I started to swoon and foam at the mouth. 'Shaindele, Shaindele.' I almost convinced myself! At that time Morris was my message boy. So Yankele, why did I ask you to deliver messages to Shaindele? You think I didn't know what was going on? That's the way I planned it! I wanted to be betrayed! I needed another ingredient for the *kasheh* I was cooking. So I made myself a victim and added a pinch of tragedy! And who can remember how many times I scolded myself? 'For Shaindele everything is a joke. But Yankele? He doesn't even know that his part was already prepared for him.' But what could I do? Could I stop the play in the middle of the performance? So I let the show go on! And while you and Shaindele were in the Catskills, I sat in my room and rejoiced! And I worked myself into such a rage, that the walls shook, and the bedbugs stayed inside their lair for a week. And when I spit in your face, you think I didn't know the whole Cafeteria was watching? I rehearsed the same scene maybe a thousand times. I even knew where the spit would land! But you didn't play out your part! I marched out of the Cafeteria expecting you to chase after me. I waited inside my room for three days, but Yankel never showed up. And now the acting was over! I started talking to the bedbugs and the walls. 'Granted! I'm the *nudnik* who caused all the trouble. But Yankel doesn't know. Suppose it was the real thing. I didn't have the right to spit in his face? This is how a friend behaves! I send him over as my emissary, and he becomes his own agent! I'll give him one more day.' Yankel, if you had only knocked on my door, I would have growled for a minute, and then kissed your hand, and said, 'Yankele, now it's your turn to spit. I insist!' But you never knocked! And I kept walking back and forth across the room. I cursed myself. 'Dope, run over to the Cafeteria, and tell Yankel the whole story. Run, before you do something drastic and it will be too late. Pincus, give up your *mishegas!*' Yankele, *kill me,* I couldn't do it! That's the way I am! Pincus has his pride! Dark lines were already appearing on my forehead. All I needed was a cape and two fangs, and I could have played Dr. Jekyll and Mr. Hyde!" He holds his hands over his face. Honest to God, for a second his fingers look like claws! "A monster! Schimmel should have locked me up behind the counter. Look how much damage I did! For what? To satisfy my *mishegas!* I became Pincus the avenger! And I planned out your execution. You think I was going to hire Benya to blow off your head? This, for me, is not an execution! I wanted to damage you in another way. Who needed bombs? Pincus had his reviews! So I attacked you every opportunity I had! First, only with little gestures, and then I devoted entire columns to Yankel and his talents! After the second review, I knew that I was making a mistake. But there was already a *dybbuk* inside me. I couldn't stop! Yankele, look at me. I'm an evil man!" His nose starts to twitch, and the boil bounces up and down. "I figured that all the *schlemiels* from the Cafeteria would collect near the counter, and after they read my reviews, Schimmel would stand up and say, 'The man is torturing himself. He wants Yankele to forgive him.' And then Schmulka would chime in. 'Look! Every word is a message to Yankel. It's a regular love story!' Did I expect them to study my reviews like the Torah? Did I think Schmulka would turn out to be another Maimonides?" He slaps the side of his head. The Flit gun and the apple with the old man's head bounce towards the footboard and land on the patched knees of Pincus' union suit. "Even Maurie had more sense than me! Yankele, when I sat across from you in the Cafeteria all these years, you think I didn't want to run over to your table, and put my head in your lap and cry! But instead, I played out my part. The victim! How many times did I feel the bump on my back press down and try to push me over to your side of the Cafeteria. I resisted! 'Wait, he'll come over to me!' Yankel, your Pincus is a fraud! Go, report back to the Cafeteria. Schimmel loves exposés." He pulls the collar of his nightshirt over his chin. *"Nu?* Let me remain with my misery."

"Pincus," I say, "Duvie should have let you play Berkowitz for life! You would have been perfect for the part! *Mommenu,* could that man tell a story!"

"What?" Pincus says, and his face pinches together like a prune. I grab his wrists. "Midget, tell me again that you never loved Shaindele!"

He bends his neck, and now his nose is parallel to the floor. "Okay! I liked her. I liked her a little. But what I said before, Yankele, it was all true." I release his wrists. He's crying again. Can I help myself? I'm crying too! "Yankele, whatever happened, it was all madness—*mishegas!* We were both maniacs." He winks to me. The whole left side of his face starts to cave in! "Yankele, a little *schnapps?*" Now he searches for his bottle. He pats all the bumps on the bed and looks under each leg of the union suit. "Who can remember where I put the *schnapps?* Maybe the bedbugs stole it!" He flits across the room like a gremlin on the lam! The night-shirt clings to his knees. He bends over the Pepsi-Cola bottle. Half his body disappears. The Pepsi-Cola bottle wavers for a second, then thinks it over, and decides not to topple.

"Pincus," I say, "forget the *schnapps.* Get dressed!"

His head emerges. Even his crumpled behind starts to frown. "I should dress myself? For what? I'm not taking a step from the room."

"Pincus, you hear? I'm taking you back to the Cafeteria."

He starts to stall. "Yankel," he says, "how is Irving?"

What, you think I don't know his tactics? "Midget," I answer him, "believe me, Irving should have remained on your knee. I liked him better when he played Hershele. *Nu?* Get dressed!"

"Hershele," he says, "Hershele." The boil on his nose is getting ready to glow. What, is he preparing a sermon for me? "Yankel, why did I sit Irving on my knee? Ask me! You think I wanted to entertain the Cafeteria? All right, it gave me an opportunity to be an actor, but

Irving wasn't the only one who could have played Hershele's part! Wolf's nephew, Bindele, was already a professional. Why didn't I pick him? Yankel, you don't know? Irving was my accomplice! We both performed for you! Did I ever call for Irving when Yankele wasn't in the Cafeteria? Could I go over and write on Schimmel's wall: 'Yankel is for me my only friend.' They would laugh at me. So whatever I had to say to you, I told to Hershele. And when I said, 'Hershele, your father is a *nudnik,* and a dope. Schimmel should throw him out of the Cafeteria,' what did it mean?" He closes both eyes. "It meant," he says, "without Yankel, Schimmel can keep his Cafeteria! Yankele, every message to Hershele was meant for you!"

You see! Who else could use such tactics! "Pincus, put on your *gatkehs* and let's go!"

He picks up the Pepsi-Cola bottle. The bottle is bigger than his head. "Yankel, walk away from me."

Honest to God, my sides are ready to split. "Look at him! Now he thinks he's Dane Clark! Pincus, who needs Duvie? I'll sign you up myself!"

Now the bottle embarrasses him. He throws it on the bed. "Yankel, don't ask me again. I'm finished with the Cafeteria. I wasted enough time with *nudniks.*" His eyebrows start to dance. "Pincus is writing a play!" He stands in front of the bed and points to the notebook and the pen. He tries to expand his sunken chest. What can he do? Even the hump on his back refuses to budge! I don't have to inspect the notebook. I know what I'll find! And only Pincus could use a pen without a point! You think he's ready to give up? He needs a little time to recuperate. He picks up the Flit gun and starts to spray the

walls. The cockroaches ignore him completely. "Yankele."
His voice starts to crack. The Flit gun knocks against
his knees. He tries again. "Yankele, the whole play is in
my head. I'm working now on the second act. I'm making
arrangements with Braverman. He's ready to reopen the
National. Only for me! A sequel, a sequel to *Muttel the
Thief*. Secunda is busy. Otherwise he would write the
music. Yankel, without Finkelstein, how can we locate
for you a suit with padded shoulders?"

Should I call him a *meshuggina* and run out of the
room? Why should I mix myself up with his *mishegas?*
What can I do? My knees are shaking! "Pincus," I say,
"leave it to me! I'll do all the casting. We'll let Schmulka
play Shimion the philosopher. And Berkowitz?" His fingers start to fidget. He tucks them under his nightshirt.
"What can we do? Who can bring Menashe back from
the West Coast! Pincus, you're elected!" You think we
need a prompter? We both start to cry at the same time.
Honest to God, I'm ready to kiss the boil on his nose.
Maybe Selma is right. Pincus' fairy! "Midget, don't waste
my time! Put on your *gatkehs,* before I tie the legs around
your neck!"

"Yankel, how can I go back to the Cafeteria?
Schmulka will laugh at me!"

"Pincus, don't worry. We'll make our entrance together!"

I help him put on the union suit. The ankle bands
reach down to his toes. "Yankele, don't make me go!
Pincus is ashamed! I don't have any more stories to tell."
What, I have to button for him his fly?

"Pincus, shut up!"

"Let Turgenev tell his own stories! Pushkin? Lermontov? I'm disowning them all!" The man doesn't have a clean shirt to his name. And all his ties are eaten up with moth holes. A market for Mendel! I cash clothes! Yankel is crying again! Today is Sunday, no? So I open his closet and take out his Sunday suit. I search every pocket for beetles. I chase the cockroaches away from his mirror and wipe it for him with my sleeve. He puts on the suit, and for the first time he looks like a *mensch*. What do you expect? Believe me, a suit from Finkelstein could turn the biggest *schlemiel* into a prince! After all, I should know! He complains that the sleeves are too short. He makes me polish all the buttons. Now he wants to brush his teeth.

"Pincus," I say, "put the toothbrush in your pocket. Who has time!" A butler I had to become? Never again! I wrap his toothbrush in some toilet paper. He wants his tweezers too! Oy, I'll have to borrow Mendele's pushcart to carry all his supplies. "Pincus, let's go!" I drag him towards the door. Now he has to say goodbye to the room. He goes through a whole routine. He bows to the bed. He winks to every wall. He even says a few words to the toilet seat. *Mommenu*, is this a case! *"Nu?"* I say, "You forgot the beetles and the bedbugs."

He pinches his lips together. "I need them here? Let them board with someone else!"

We march out of the room. He doesn't even bother to close the door. "What can they steal? My toilet seat? Yankel, make a move. The whole Cafeteria is waiting for me." Go figure him out! He flies down the steps like a loon. What can I do? I follow him!

11.

——

Showdown
at
Schimmel's

——

As soon as we cross Houston Street, Pincus switches gears. He wants to go back. "Yankele, I can't face them. What can I do?" I slap his behind. "Midget, march!" Honest to God, I'll drive him like a donkey! He tells me to leave his behind alone. He can walk by himself. He stumbles across the street. His whole body is out of order. His elbows jerk in different directions. One knee disobeys the other. And his toes act like they're ready to run off with his shoes. You expect him to collapse in the middle of the street?—believe me, you don't know Pincus! He starts cursing his arms and his legs. "My friends," he says, "you'll go where *I* want you to go!" And right away he puts an end to the mutiny. His elbows jerk now in one direction. His knees obey all his commands, and

his toes are prisoners again inside his Florsheim shoes.
Now that he's the master, he can afford to mumble to
himself. "Schimmel, you should only have my constipa-
tion! Schmulka, hide behind your bench. Pincus is on the
warpath! Look who they gave me for an escort! *Yankel!*"
He puts one hand near his throat and discovers something
for himself. He's ready to kill me. I mean it! "This is the
way you dressed me? How can I sit in the Cafeteria
without a tie?" Should I paddle him? "March!" He
curses me with every step. But when we arrive on Second
Avenue, Pincus becomes Pincus again. He knows that
someone from the Cafeteria could be watching him. He
forces air into his sunken chest, and starts to strut. The
hump on his back is already bristling. He even puts his
behind on parade. Wolf is waiting outside Moskowitz and
Lupowitz. He's without his balalaika. He runs over to
Pincus and starts to dance up and down. Me he ignores.
"A miracle!" They kiss each other on the cheek. Pincus
backs off. "Please," he says, "not in public!"

"Wolf," I say, "you gave up the Cafeteria? This is
your new hangout?"

Now he notices me! "Yankel, Schmulka stationed
me here. I'm on patrol!"

"Patrol?" Pincus says, "for what are you patrolling?"

"Farbstein!"

"What," I say, "he bought off the mortgage? The Cafeteria is closing down? Now Fishie will sit in jail for life!"

Wolf throws up his hands. "Yankel, you don't know?
Fishie is sitting in the Cafeteria. With Tillie! She bailed
him out. Sure, first she emptied out Farbstein's drawer.
And when Farbstein finds out, will be murder! He'll
storm the Cafeteria. So Schmulka put me on patrol."

Let the spider come, I'm ready to dance in the street.
Fishie, Fishie. *Nu?* Tillie bailed him out! What, if I made
twenty more tries, you think I would get anywhere? What
can you expect from a player? I threaten and I shout.
I put on a terrific show, but nothing happens. Leave it
to Tillie! All she needs is one try! Tell me, what made
her change her mind?

Right away Pincus takes over. "Wolf," he says, "stay
here!" Honest to God, Wolf is ready to salute him! "And
remember. Next time, no talking when you're on patrol.
Yankel, come. Leave Farbstein to me!" What can you
do? The midget is in command! Even his elbows are
afraid of him. We march over to the Cafeteria. Oy, they
barricaded the door. Tables, chairs, borscht bottles. And
who do you think is standing behind the barricade with
a cleaver in one hand and a salami sandwich in the other?
Schmulka! And with him is Mendele. He's still wearing
his patch. Schmulka sees me and Pincus standing together, and he rocks his head back and forth. The cleaver
almost drops out of his hand. "Oy," he says, "the *nudniks*
are united again. Now I'll never have peace!"

Pincus wags one finger. "Schmulka, break up the barricade."

And how does Schmulka answer him? *"Meshuggina,"*
he says, "Farbstein is on the way. Who knows how many
troops he's bringing with him! He owns the whole police
force. And he'll make one call to the armory, and the
National Guard will show up!"

The midget marches up to the door. "Schmulka! Farbstein belongs to me. Move!"

Schmulka wants to protest, but he knows he's no match
for the midget. So he stands behind his chair, and starts

pleading with me. What does he want from my life? First he finishes off his salami sandwich, then he shows me his battle plans, and talks about invasions, and troop movements, and commando tactics—where did he pick up such *mishegas?* From Schimmel?—and finally he slaps his sides and clears away all the tables, chairs, and borscht bottles. The cleaver he keeps! Pincus stands under the doorway. He notices the patch over Mendele's eye. *"Nu?"* he says, "what happened to the merchant? Mendele? No smile? No hello? All right, nobody expects you to be a philosopher. But show me you're alive! Even a curse is good enough. Mendele?" The midget smiles. He even allows his lips to part. "Mendele?" When the midget works on you his magic, who can resist him? Honest to God, the man could charm a Golem or a Frankenstein! Crazy or not, Mendele doesn't have a chance! He smiles back. His closed eye also answers the midget. The patch bounces up and down. Now the midget begins to modulate his voice. "Mendele, come here." You think he needs a flute? How can you compare a piper to Pincus? What, did the Pied Piper have a boil on his nose? Maybe he had a costume with a hundred different colors, but believe me, he never wore Finkelstein's a suit! Let the Piper pipe all he wants, next to Pincus he's nothing! Mendele's body warms to the magic in Pincus' voice. His fingers are ready to fly. The patch drops down and Pincus stares at Mendele's eye. His voice strains for a second. "Mendele?" Mendel's body stiffens. He cups both hands over the eye and runs behind his pushcart. He's crying. I can see his back move up and down. "I cash . . ."

"See!" Schmulka says, "that's Farbstein's work! The

landlord threw him out, and Mendele ran around with his pushcart like one of Gogol's ghosts! Who knows if we'll ever be able to put him together again."

Pincus sticks out his nose. He aims the boil at Schmulka. "Farbstein threw him out? How come nobody told me?"

Now it's Schmulka's turn. He puts his paunch in front of the midget's chin. "You hear him? Midget! How many times did I knock on your door? Did it help? 'Schimmel is on a hunger strike. Mendele is out in the street.' My neck is sore from all the shouting."

Pincus pulls back his nose. Even the boil retreats! "Nobody protected him? Yankele, *you?* Irving?"

What can I say? "Midget . . . "

Schmulka cuts me off. "Yankele, you have to make apologies to him yet? Where was *he?*—the *president* of the Cafeteria! He locked himself up in his room. What, if the midget stuck around, you think Farbstein would have started up? Just because he's a bastard, it doesn't mean he's a dope. Midget, you'll boil your own potatoes!"

Pincus walks over to the pushcart. If you ask me, his elbows are ready for another mutiny. He tries to keep them locked against his sides. His whole body starts to jerk. "Mendele?" Mendel sits in the pushcart with a bunch of borscht bottles. The midget works on him with his voice. Mendel doesn't hear a word. What can you do? The man lost his magic! "Wait," he says, "Farbstein will pay through the nose." He bangs into a table. Schmulka looks at me. We bring the midget over to the back of the Cafeteria. Fishie and Tillie are sitting near Schimmel's community toilet. Honest to God, they're holding hands. And Tillie is still wearing her steel brassière. Oy, her

cantaloupes cover half the table! She sees the midget
walking between me and Schmulka. "Pincus!" she says.
"Now the Cafeteria is complete!" Fishie is drinking a
glass of tea. He dangles two tea bags with his free hand.
Don't laugh, it's a complicated job! He winks to me. He
brings both eyebrows down for a second, and half his
face disappears. Eyebrows he has? Two cliffs!

"Fishie," I say, *"mazel tov!"* We shake hands over the
tea bags. "Fishie, what, I made any progress with all my
talk? If you had to depend on Yankel, you would still
be sitting in jail. Who should know that all the time
Tillie was a secret agent for the Cafeteria!" Tillie's cheeks
are red, and believe me, it's not from her rouge! One
of her cantaloupes slides down, and without making a
tzimis, she puts it back in its right place. Tell me, where
can you find another Tillie! "Yankel," she says, "I had
to learn my lesson, no? How could I survive without the
Cafeteria?" She squeezes Fishie's hand.

"Yankel," Fishie says, "where's Benya?"

What, you want me to tell Fishie that Benya ran out
on him? Better he shouldn't have to hear the truth! *Nu?*
So what can I tell him? Yankele, *quick,* make up a story!
And for once, Farbstein comes in handy! "Benya? Fishie,
Farbstein sent the police after him, so Benya ran uptown.
Don't worry, he'll be back! He was ready to bomb the
tombs. Honest to God! But Farbstein interrupted all his
plans."

Now Pincus gets into the act. He puts one fist on top
of the other. "When the landlord shows up, leave him
to me."

"Pincus," Schmulka says, "battles are not for you.
That's my department! Sit down better and tell us a story.

I have to plan a new attack. *Nu?* Turgenev? Tolstoy? Take your pick."

When Tillie hears the name Turgenev, both of her cantaloupes start to bounce. But the midget refuses. He's not in the mood. "No more stories," he says. "Pincus is retiring."

"What?" Schmulka says. "Midget, the Cafeteria doesn't take in pikers and retired story-tellers. Everybody has to produce. You expect Schimmel to feed you for free?" Schmulka slaps his face with both hands. "I forgot all about him! *Schimmel,*" he says, *"Schimmel.* Who knows if he survived his hunger strike!" He runs behind the counter. "Yankel, you knock! Me he'll never believe." What, I have to spend my whole life knocking on other people's doors? Should I tell him no? Schmulka, knock yourself! I walk over to Schimmel's door. "Schimmel, come out. The midget is here!" I knock three times. "Schimmel? Honest to God, he's here!"

"Yankel, it's no use. Pincus is the only one! Midget, serenade him!"

Pincus walks over to his table. He inspects the salt shakers. He knows that everyone is watching him. He holds out one hand. "Schimmel, out!"

Who knows? Somebody gave him back his magic! The door opens right away. Schimmel comes out. You should see him! His shoulders are stooped like a monkey. Believe it or not, his nose almost touches the ground! The man can hardly walk. His left foot refuses to follow the right. He leans against the counter and rubs his eyes. Maybe he's a little blind from staying so long in the dark. Pincus poses himself. He stands with a salt shaker in each hand. Nobody says a word. Schimmel puts on his apron.

His fingers can still tie a knot. He sings to himself. Then he starts to growl. "Schmulka, prepare the borscht." He watches the midget with one eye. "And be careful when you cook the potatoes." Pincus sits down. Schmulka starts to complain. "Everybody expects me to be his servant!" He mimics Schimmel. " 'Prepare the borscht!' I'll take my bench and move over to Rapoport's." This already is like old times. The Cafeteria is back to normal. All we need is Wolf and his balalaika. Oy, I had to open up my big mouth! Wolf marches in. His jaw hangs down and he's ready to spit out his teeth. He reports to Pincus' table. "Farbstein is coming!"

What can you do? You expect Schimmel's to last forever? Let the Cafeteria crumble! I'll run uptown and live with Lena! What about Pincus? Don't worry, I'll take him with me. Maybe Lena will find another widow for him. Who knows, we'll throw Kapel out, and take over the whole Center. Yankel, *mishegas!*

"Farbstein," Wolf says, "Farbstein!"

Schmulka abandons the borscht. He looks all over for his cleaver. "The landlord brought with him his army?"

"No. He's alone."

"What," Schmulka says, "he expects to leave the Cafeteria alive?"

Tillie nudges Fishie's arm. They walk over to Pincus' table and stand behind the midget. Tillie's lips are parched. She puts one hand on Pincus' chair. Fishie has to sit down. He rubs his swollen leg. "Yankel," he says, "whatever happens, I'm not going back to the tombs. They'll have to carry me out in a box."

Nu? We sit and wait for the landlord to make his

entrance. Schimmel's Commandoes! Maybe a fire escape will fall on him? Oy, I can already see his bald head through Schimmel's unwashed window. Enter Farbstein. He's wearing his black suit. You think he came without his notebook? He holds it close to his chest like a shield. He halts near the door. Pincus he didn't expect! He writes something down in his notebook. He must be making a list. Sure, he'll condemn the whole Cafeteria! I watch his pencil jump. Now he walks towards the midget's table. The linoleum crackles under his feet. He passes Mendele's pushcart. Mendel offers him a borscht bottle. "My finest merchandise. Here, take a sample." Farbstein refuses him. He watches us with his spidery eyes. Tillie holds my hand. Her body is shaking. Farbstein points one of his crooked fingers at her. The finger should only fall off!

"This is how you repay my kindness? Who took you off the street and bought you pocketbooks and shoes? What, I slapped you or pulled out your hair? I didn't give you enough to eat?" Listen to him! He expects yet sympathy from the Cafeteria. Oy, I would like to answer him! 'Tillie you took off the street, hah? Who threw her out in the first place! Snake! Skunk!' Don't worry, Tillie can talk for herself! First she moves closer to Fishie. "Farbstein," she says, "if Tillie Moskowitz lives with somebody, it has to be a *mensch,* not a mole!"

The landlord drops his notebook. His bald head jumps up and down. "Wait," he says, "they have quarters for women too in the tombs! I'll make sure the bailiff throws away the key." He picks up the notebook. Honest to God, I'm ready to trip him. But who wants to make more trouble for Tillie! You think Fishie is going to let Farbstein threaten her? "Farbstein," he says, "make one wrong move, and I'll nail you to the wall!"

Farbstein starts to laugh. Half his rotten teeth stick out. "Look, the Lone Ranger! Fishbein, listen to me. You won't be sitting here for long. I can give you my personal guarantee. Schimmel will have to ship out lunch boxes for you to Sing Sing. And Yankel, you can stand on your head, Irving will never help him out." He stabs his chest with one thumb. "I pick out for him all his clients."

Schmulka puts on top of the counter two hard-boiled eggs, a bruised tomato, and an apple that's covered with warts. "Schimmel, give me the word!"

Schimmel looks at the landlord. "What does he want? —cash?"

"I want the fifteen hundred dollars she stole for the gangster's bail!"

Schimmel puts both elbows on the counter. "Fifteen hundred dollars? Schmulka, can we afford it? We'll have to give up the Cafeteria!"

Pincus bangs the table with his tiny fists. The salt shakers start to dance. "Schimmel, don't pay out a cent. Farbstein, walk away! Garbage you'll collect, not fifteen hundred dollars! If Tillie is indicted, and Fishie has to go back to jail, I'll organize the whole East Side. We'll picket every house. You think your supers will stick with you? They'll break all your boilers! You'll have to move your office to Pitkin Avenue. Farbstein, for your sake, don't start up with the Cafeteria. We'll all eat you alive."

"The Cafeteria, hah?" Farbstein hunches over one shoulder and writes down two words. "Wait! I'll bring

back with me half the precinct. Wait! I'll arrest the whole
Cafeteria!" He opens his jacket and shows us his badge.
"You think I'm not a member of the auxiliary police?
Wait!" He holds out both hands. "Ten minutes! You'll
hear the sirens, don't worry. The whole Cafeteria. Everybody! You'll all go for a ride." He points to the pushcart.
"That idiot too! With all his junk!" He starts laughing
to himself and walks towards the door. Mendele rocks
the pushcart. "Bastard," he cries, "bring me back my
merchandise." Not even a Golem could resist such a
cry! Farbstein's narrow shoulders draw together. His
hands withdraw inside his sleeves. He turns around, says,
"Wait," and walks outside. The pushcart's prow starts
to tilt. "I cash clothes . . ." Schimmel wheels Mendele
over to Pincus' table. *"Shah!"*

Schmulka comes out from behind the counter. "Oy,
we have to put back the barricade. Yankel, Fishie, arm
yourselves. Everybody, pick up a broom. Wolf, *nu?* Go
back to your station. Find out how big an army Farbstein
has. Go!" Wolf waits for Pincus to give him the word.

"Wolf," Pincus says, "pick out a chair and sit.
Schmulka, bring over his balalaika."

"Midget," Schmulka shouts, "Farbstein is preparing
to invade the Cafeteria, and you ask for music? Mendele,
you're the normal one, not him!"

"Schmulka, the balalaika!" Schmulka slaps his sides
and walks behind the counter. His head disappears for a
minute. Then the balalaika's long neck starts to slide
over the edge of the counter. Like a spook! Wolf catches
the balalaika before it falls, and brings it back to his seat.
He plays with the pegs attached to the balalaika's midget-
sized head. Schmulka leans over the counter. "Pincus,

please. Let me put a table in front of the door. *One* table! I have a plan. I can attach a hose to Schimmel's vats, and make a regular bazooka! We can all stand behind the counter and spray borscht at them for an hour."

"Schmulka, save your bazooka for another time. Let Farbstein bring as many armies as he wants. He knows where he can find us."

"What, you want to give up the Cafeteria without a fight? Midget, go back to your room! Yankele? Help me out! Put me in charge! Schimmel? You know Farbstein wants revenge. He'll make sure they wreck the whole Cafeteria. Listen to me! Wolf, put away the balalaika and walk over to the door. Oy, I can hear the sirens already!"

The midget stands up. His chest bangs against the edge of the table. The ketchup bottle almost reaches his chin. "Schmulka, I'll take you in the back and tie you to Schimmel's toilet seat. I mean it! Farbstein wants us to panic. Then he'll have for himself a free show. No! We'll sit and wait. Wolf, play!"

Wolf is a little nervous. He hasn't played for Pincus in over a month. The balalaika sits in his lap. He stares at the finger board and then starts to strum. *Tum Balalaika*. Pincus closes one eye and hums to himself. Tillie sits on the table and sings. "Tum bala, tum bala, tum balalai . . ." Her cantaloupes kiss the midget's head. Schimmel watches some smoke rise over the counter. "Schmulka, you forgot about the potatoes!" He runs behind the counter. "Barricades he worries about. Schmulka, if the potatoes are black, I'll barricade your head!" Mendele sits in the pushcart and rocks his shoulders in time to the music. Gershen the Gonef comes into the Cafeteria. Who can believe it? The Gonef left his

stand! A few of the *nudniks* from Tepper's candy store
are bunched behind him. Gershen congratulates himself.
"See! I knew it all the time. Pincus is back!" They all
congregate around the midget's table. Schmulka curses
everybody and lights Pincus' cigar. Schimmel brings over
the potatoes and the borscht. One or two of the potatoes
are already charred. Schimmel starts to peel their broken
skins. He makes Schmulka blow on all the potatoes.
Schmulka's cheeks start to swell. I volunteer to take over
his job. Schmulka whispers in my ear. "Yankele, you
think it was a bluff? Maybe Farbstein won't come."

"Who knows?" I say, and I blow on the last potato.
Pincus pretends that the potatoes are sour, but he gives
himself away. The boil on his nose starts to blush. We
wait around him like little children. He knows what we
want. First he finishes his borscht! Wolf doesn't need a
signal. He puts the balalaika away. Pincus starts to pity
himself. "They won't even let me retire! Am I a machine?
You think you can turn me on and out comes a story?
Wolf, pick up your balalaika and play. How can I tell
a story after eating burned potatoes? No, Pincus is not
in the mood." What can he do? Again his nose gives him
away. Honest to God, the boil is already on fire! What,
he wants us to go down on our knees? Let him keep his
stories! I'll go back to my old seat in the corner. He
sees me leave his circle. Right away he calls me over.
"Yankele," he says, "you won't even allow me a little
pleasure? After twenty-five years!" Does he think he's the
only actor in the place? I start to fidget in front of his
face. He mumbles something to himself. The man has to
warm up, no? *Nu?* Will it be Gogol today? The midget
watches the way Tillie and Fishie are holding hands,

then he touches his boil, and announces to the Cafeteria: *"Turgenev!"* Oy, the opera singer again! Who can
remember her name? Tillie's whole face starts to glow,
under the wrinkles and the rouge! "Turgenev," she says,
"Turgenev." Schimmel stands over me. "Yankel," he
says, "I can hear them coming. It's a regular invasion!"
Who's listening to him? *"Shah,"* I say, *"shah."* Soon the
midget will go through all the contortions, and show us
Turgenev with his swollen cheeks and clumsy hands, and
the opera singer with her empty chest and burning eyes.
Then he'll take us with Turgenev across half the countries
in Europe, and the whole Cafeteria will be chasing after
the prima donna. He'll scold Turgenev a little. *"Nudnik,"*
he'll call him. "What, every princess in Kiev and Peters-
burg ran after him, and he wanted only his opera singer!"
Don't worry, the way he tells the story, you'll fall in love
with her too! Maybe Schimmel will dedicate another
chair. For the prima donna! And the Cafeteria will have
a new sweetheart! And at least for a little while I won't
have to think about Farbstein, and Irving, and Maurie
the Meshuggina! And Fishie will forget about his swollen leg and his room in Raymond Street. And I know.
Even Mendele will relax. He won't have time to worry
about his merchandise. He'll sit in the pushcart and mimic
the midget's every move. *Shah!* Pincus is ready to begin!
He slaps his thighs, raises one of his crooked eyebrows,
and says, "Turgenev? What was he? . . ." Mendele puts
away his borscht bottles. Gershen stops staring at Tillie's
cantaloupes. I move my chair closer to the table. "Turgenev," Schimmel says to himself. Schmulka watches
the door.

About the Author

Jerome Charyn is twenty-six years old and was graduated from Columbia College in 1959. He has taught English in New York at the High School of Music and Art and at the High School of Performing Arts. He is currently studying Russian at Columbia University under a National Defense Fellowship. He has published short stories in *Commentary* and *Mademoiselle*, and is now at work on a new novel and a collection of short stories.